Ties That Bind Her

APPLEMAN'S GAP
BOOK TWO

KELLY UTT

2024 Standards of Starlight Paperback Edition

www.standardsofstarlight.com

Cover art by Elizabeth Mackey

ISBN: 978-1-952893-29-2

While many of the locations in this book are true to life, some details of the setting have been changed.

Appleman's Gap is a fictional town, set about an hour east of Nashville, Tennessee on the edge of the Cumberland Plateau. I envision it much like the mountainous region of the Appalachians in East Tennessee, but placed closer to Nashville. It's a small town along a winding river that empties into a picturesque lake with a bustling marina. Apple orchards line the hillsides and a railroad skirts the river bank.

Nashville, of course, is a real town, the bustling, creative capital of the U.S. state of Tennessee. Our characters in the Appleman's Gap series often go to Nashville since the fictional town is considered to be within the Nashville metro area. Like the real-life Nashville metro area, Appleman's Gap is experiencing rapid growth with new residents moving in and new construction happening everywhere.

Ties That Bind Her is a work of fiction. Any references to historical events, real people, or real places are used fictitiously. Other names, characters, places, and events are products of my imagination, and any resemblance to actual events or places or persons, living or dead, is entirely coincidental.

Thanks for reading,
Kelly Utt

PART ONE

Hidden in Plain Sight

IT WAS STILL dark outside when Laurel's phone rang. She groaned, then rolled away from Brad and reached for the device on her nightstand. Lilly stirred at their feet. The winter's chill had left beads of condensation on the windows, yet they were warm and cozy inside the bungalow.

"Let it ring," Brad said, his voice heavy with sleep.

"Have you forgotten what we do for a living?" Laurel asked. "We don't have that luxury."

He scooted close and kissed the back of her neck, gently moving her long, wavy hair out of the way as he did. "You're still on leave. Which means, you're still all mine."

"Oh, I'm all yours, all right," she cooed, "but I have to answer the phone." Her tone became even more serious when she saw the caller ID on the screen. "It's Jimmy."

Laurel's Special Agent in Charge at the Bureau, Jimmy Paulson, had returned to Washington, D.C. after Baby Jasper had been found safe, but Laurel knew that wasn't the end of her boss' business in Appleman's Gap. The Cradler, the head of the kidnapping syndicate responsible for the baby's disappearance, was still out there somewhere. Presumably, he was still up to no good. Despite the F.B.I.'s best efforts, they didn't have a positive ID on the criminal, let alone know where to find him.

"What?" Laurel breathed as she picked up the phone.

Laurel and Jimmy were friends. They didn't have to act overly formal with each other. At least, not unless his superiors were listening. That didn't happen often.

"Well, good morning to you, Sunshine," Jimmy quipped. "You always were a grouch this time of day. I'm glad I'm not there to experience it in person."

"It's 5 a.m. What do you want?"

He didn't hesitate. "Are you ready to come back to work?"

Brad's morning body was becoming aroused as he caressed Laurel. He slid a hand under her nightshirt, stopping to admire the growing bump in her lower abdomen. Laurel was well into her second trimester now. Brad had even been able to feel the baby kick with regularity. He found his fiancé sexier than ever while she was pregnant.

She shooed him off as she focused her attention on what Jimmy was saying. "I don't know," she replied. "Why?"

"Because a woman's body was found last night in Cedar Hollow. It looks like a baby had been cut out of her womb." His pace slowed as he said the words, almost like he didn't want them to leave his mouth.

"My God," Laurel mumbled. The thought made her physically sick.

She'd become soft lately, and she knew it. She wasn't sure she was cut out to be an F.B.I. agent anymore. Especially now that she was becoming a mom.

Her reaction got Brad's attention. "What is it?" he asked.

"Hold on, Jimmy," Laurel said. "I'm putting you on speaker."

She pushed the button, so that Brad could hear, too.

"Hey, Brad," Jimmy said solemnly.

"Hey, man," Brad replied. "I take it you aren't calling with good news."

"I wish I was, but I'm afraid not."

"A woman's mutilated body was found," Laurel said, filling Brad in. "Cedar Hollow."

Brad stiffened. As an area outside of Appleman's Gap, that was his jurisdiction. "How am I just hearing about this?" he asked.

"Our people found the body," Jimmy explained. "They were following a lead in the woods when they stumbled upon it. Since the Bureau is handling the search for The Cradler, there was no reason to call in local police. I'm informing you now, as a courtesy."

Brad didn't like that, but he understood. He grunted his reply, then turned his attention back to the warm sensation of Laurel next to him in bed. He pulled her closer, aware that the news of a body in the nearby woods would be upsetting.

"They think a baby was ... *cut* out of her womb," Laurel said, hesitating over the gruesome word.

"That's terrible," Brad said, placing a protective hand over their own baby.

She nodded. "Jimmy wants to know if I'm ready to go back to work."

"Why now, Jimmy?" Brad asked.

Jimmy seemed reluctant to push the matter. After all, he cared about Laurel as a friend. He knew she wasn't at the top of her game as Agent Dane right now. Being pregnant while a kidnapping syndicate was stealing the spotlight and then finding out that her father was alive had been a lot to take in. Jimmy assumed that Laurel hadn't processed it all yet. He was right.

"Look, if I could lead the investigation myself from down there, I would," Jimmy said.

"So get on a plane."

"I'm at home in D.C., though," Jimmy continued, "and I'm supposed to leave for Antigua in two days to see my wife's little brother get married. My wife will kill me if I'm not there for his big day."

"What about your agents, Samira and Malik?" Brad tried.

Brad and Laurel could almost hear Jimmy shrug through the phone. "They're good agents, but they're green. They aren't ready to take the lead on this."

They sat in silence for a moment. "So, you want me to take the lead?" Laurel asked.

"You've done it dozens of times," Jimmy replied. "Just another day's work."

It was so much more than that.

"You know, Jimmy," Laurel said, "we're supposed to travel to South Carolina to visit my dad today. I haven't seen him since Jasper was returned. I wasn't ready until now. Brad, Mikey, and I are all driving down together. The trip has been planned for weeks."

Jimmy was growing frustrated. Technically, he could get tough and insist that Laurel return to work. He was still her boss, after all. She'd have no real choice but to either follow instructions, or resign her position and turn in her badge. He didn't want to see the latter happen, though, and he was afraid it might.

"Look," Jimmy said, "imagine it was you who was brutally murdered. Your baby cut out of its safe place in your womb. Both of your lives ended too soon at the hands of a vicious madman."

"Jesus, Jimmy," Brad said. "Easy."

"All I'm saying is, wouldn't you want someone to prevent the same thing from happening to anyone else? Wouldn't you want to bring the perpetrator to justice? See him locked up?"

"How do you know it's a male?" Brad asked.

"Because most perpetrators of violent crimes are," Laurel replied. "You know that."

Brad nodded, nuzzling the back of her neck.

"Hey, man," Brad said after a pause, "how about you give us a while to talk it over?"

"I don't need—" Laurel began, but Brad held up a finger to stop her.

Jimmy sighed heavily. "You're my only option, Dane. *Please.* I can set your dad up in a safe house nearby. Bring him to you."

Laurel brightened at that news. "You have one around here?"

"Of course. I can have it ready to go by sundown. He can stay as long as he likes. In fact, he might be able to help with some behind-the-scenes investigation. After what happened to you as a kid, he's champing at the bit to take these guys down."

The memories from that trauma were still in fragments. They had been buried so deep for so long, they seemed like they'd take some time to reveal themselves in the light of day.

Jimmy had offered to connect Laurel with a psychologist at the Bureau who could help. She'd need to be back in D.C. to see anyone in person, though. She wasn't at all ready to go there. Especially since she and Brad were happy right here in Appleman's Gap.

"That might work," Brad said. "If your dad could come here, we could hang out with him as time allows while also hunting the killer."

Laurel still hadn't taken her fiancé and her boss to task for not telling her that her father was alive. She'd wanted to do that when they were all together, in person. The wait was driving her crazy, though. She was angry with all three of them for keeping such important information from her. Her mom was angry, too, but Maureen was too wrapped up with Mack Roberts to properly converse about the situation. That discussion would have to happen at a later date.

Jimmy made encouraging sounds on the other end of the phone. "Exactly," he said. "It's a win-win."

Just then, they heard a loud bang from the back of the house. It sounded like glass breaking. Lilly leaped up, barking furiously. Before they could stop her, she bounded down from the bed and left the room.

Terror shot through Laurel. She wasn't normally so jumpy, but the news about the mutilated mother and missing baby had her on edge. The blackness outside didn't help either. It was a deep darkness, the kind that can only come in the depths of winter. The kind that cloaks criminals and allows them to do their worst. That kind of darkness paired with an unexpected sound touched on something primal in a woman's brain. She looked to Brad to protect her. At least, she did for a few seconds, before her training kicked in and she remembered that she was perfectly capable of taking care of herself.

"I'll call you back," Laurel whispered into the phone, then she disconnected the call.

Brad raised a hand to indicate that she should stay put, then he slowly reached for his service weapon in the safe within his nightstand. He didn't have to tell Laurel to be quiet. That much was understood. If there was an intruder in the house and they aimed to take Brad and Laurel by surprise, it was imperative to let them think that was a possibility. The moment the intruder let down his guard is when a counter attack would be most effective.

Brad raised his weapon as he slowly stood. He never took his eyes off the doorway, making sure to keep his body between the point of entry and the woman he loved.

Laurel saw what he was doing, and she appreciated it. Her thoughts oscillated between wanting to respond like she'd been taught at The Farm and hiding to protect their unborn child. She marveled at how quickly her worldview had changed. Another person's life depended on her now.

She and Brad made eye contact, and in that instant, a silent understanding passed between them. Laurel would make choices that would protect their baby. She had failed her nephew, Jasper, when she'd let him be taken during the carjacking. It was nothing short of a miracle that he'd been found safe. Laurel knew that it wasn't her fault. Not technically. But she still felt responsible. She could never live with herself if anything happened on her watch again. Especially not to her own baby.

Nodding, Brad motioned toward the closet. Laurel picked up a metal lamp from the nightstand on her side of the bed, then stepped inside and carefully closed the door. She didn't have a gun with her, although she desperately wished she did. She'd left hers in the bedroom at her mom's house, assuming that Brad had enough firearms to take care of them both. By the look on his face, she surmised that he had plenty of firearms—just not in this room. She hoped they were in a safe that the intruder couldn't access. Surely, Brad had all of his weapons properly secured.

Suddenly, loud music started playing, confusing Laurel and Brad. The sound was distorted. It sounded like it was coming from a phone. It took them less than a minute to recognize "Strawberry Wine" by Deanna Carter. The song had been popular when they were kids. Laurel remembered her parents dancing to it in the living room. She also remembered the part in the lyrics where it talks about thirty being old. She could only laugh, except she needed to be quiet.

"Relax," Brad said as he loosened the grip on his weapon.

"How do you know it's okay?" Laurel asked.

"Because Lilly stopped barking and nineties country can only mean one thing," he explained.

Laurel looked at him quizzically. "What?"

"Jamie Beck," Brad said, just as her voice could be heard from somewhere nearby.

"Sorry!" Jamie called sheepishly. "My bad."

Two

CORNELIUS DANE STRETCHED and wiped the sleep from his eyes, a warm mug of coffee in one hand as he stood on his back deck.

It was January, and the day was pleasant and bright with temps in the low sixties. The Lowcountry of South Carolina rarely got cold. At least, not as cold as it got back home in Appleman's Gap, Tennessee.

"Morning!" a jogger said cheerfully as he shuffled by on the beach behind the house Cornelius had been renting on Sullivan's Island. On a clear day, you could see Fort Sumter National Monument from there.

The jogger had a black lab with him, although the pup wasn't on a leash. The beach at Sullivan's Island was a popular spot for pet owners to bring their furry friends, and leashes weren't required this time of morning. Dogs delighted in the pools that formed at low tide, making it easy for them to take a dip without having to navigate the waves. The black lab ran ahead a few steps and splashed around as he waited for his owner to catch up.

"Good morning!" Cornelius called back, raising his mug. "Beautiful dog you have there."

The jogger turned to thank him, running backward for a moment.

It was a good morning. Cornelius' daughter, Laurel, and his son, Mikey, were coming to visit today. Laurel's fiancé, Brad, was tagging along, too.

It had been weeks since his two oldest children had learned he was alive. They'd needed time to process the revelation, which Cornelius had understood, especially since he'd asked them to keep his secret and not tell anyone he'd faked his own death. Their cooperation in protecting his secret was essential to the undercover work he was doing. He wouldn't be able to take down The Cradler's kidnapping syndicate unless he could work from the shadows.

Cornelius had come too far to give up now. He'd vowed not to let the villain slip through his fingers this time.

Turning to watch the black dog gallop down the beach toward Isle of Palms, Cornelius caught a glimpse of his reflection in the sliding glass door.

"Looking scruffy, old man," he mused.

In an effort to disguise his appearance, he had cut his hair shorter than usual, but it was the long, scraggly beard that continued to catch him off guard when he saw himself in the mirror. He hadn't shaved since the day of his fake funeral, when he'd watched from a distance as his family and friends had gathered to say their goodbyes. He'd known that he wouldn't remain a ghost forever, and it had pained him to think about how it would hurt his loved ones when they found out the truth. He hoped they could, eventually, forgive him.

The landline in the kitchen rang, distracting him from his thoughts.

"Hello?" Cornelius said tentatively as he set his coffee on the counter. It was early, although not as early as it was in Appleman's Gap. It had been months, but Cornelius' body still seemed wired for Central Standard Time.

He hated to answer the phone at all, but it was important that he embrace the fake identity he'd established. It needed to look completely real, in case The Cradler or his goons came sniffing around.

"May I speak with Dennis McCready?" a woman on the other end of the phone asked.

Her voice was pleasant. Nothing about it set off alarm bells, yet Cornelius had been in law enforcement long enough to know that things weren't always what they seemed. He wondered how she knew his name. Well, his fake name, anyway.

"Speaking," he said. "What can I do for you?"

"Hi, I'm Tricia Bowers. I'm president of the homeowners association here on the island. I know you're renting, but you've been here a while and I thought you might be interested in some of our social events. They're open to long-term renters, too."

She talked faster as she went. Almost like she was nervous about something. Cornelius reminded himself that he couldn't be too careful. Social events made him wary. What if he let his guard down and said something to indicate his real identity? Better to keep a low profile.

"I don't do social events. Thanks, anyway. Goodbye," he said, moving to hang up the phone.

"Wait!" Tricia exclaimed. "Don't hang up."

Cornelius paused. He'd always been a sucker for a female in distress. Once a pretty lady batted her eyelashes at him a few times, he was done for. Although he couldn't be sure, Tricia sounded pretty. If he had to guess, Cornelius would put her somewhere in her forties. Maybe early fifties, which was still well within the age range of women who caught his attention.

"Why not?" he asked, against his better judgment.

Tricia hesitated, too, but a faint tapping sound could be heard on her end. It sounded like she was tapping a finger absentmindedly, perhaps on a counter.

"Well?" Cornelius prompted. "Lady, I have things to do. If you have something to say, spit it out. Otherwise, leave me be."

"I find you attractive," she blurted.

Cornelius wrinkled his brow. How did she know what he looked like? And besides, what red-blooded woman would find him attractive with this scraggly beard? He knew the style looked fine on other men, but it was a far cry from the clean-shaven good looks he'd grown accustomed to for himself.

"That was ... forward," he said.

"Sorry," she added. "I don't usually say things like that. It's just that I've been single for so long and all the men around here are old and tired and I got excited when I saw you at your mailbox while I was driving past the other day and—"

"Slow down, please," he replied with a chuckle. "You're sweet, but you're making me tired just listening."

"I'm rambling, aren't I? I tend to do that when I'm—"

"It's okay," he said. He was quickly becoming enamored with her . Something about her flustered speech was charming. He had to admit, he knew a few tricks that would help her calm down.

"Does that mean you'll come to our neighborhood fish fry tonight? It's on the beach, down by the lighthouse. You might not know, but us locals refer to the lighthouse as Charleston Light. It's one of the most modern lighthouses in the country. I have a picture of it framed all nice in my home. Oh, I should say ... there will be more than just fish. I know for certain we'll have a mess of shrimp, too. Danny Willowby from down the lane has a shrimpin' boat and he brings fresh shrimp every year. Sometimes scallops—"

"I get it. Sure. Why not?" Cornelius replied. "What time?"

"Six o'clock."

"I have some people coming to visit. Is it okay if I bring a few with me?"

He was careful not to say that they were family.

"The more, the merrier!" Tricia chirped. "You and your guests will be welcome."

"Can we bring anything?" Cornelius asked, noticing that his tone had softened considerably since a few minutes ago when he was ready to hang up on Tricia. He'd need to tread carefully.

"You could bring some hush puppies or some okra," she said. "Or if that's too complicated, some beer or wine will do. Do you cook?"

Cornelius smiled. He did cook. In fact, it was one of his favorite pastimes. He hadn't done it since he'd been on the island, though. Without anyone to cook for, it hadn't seemed as appealing. Besides, he'd been deep into internet research most days, his head buried in his laptop as he searched for clues that would help bring The Cradler to justice.

"I cook," he said, figuring the fewer words he used, the better.

"Oh, goodie!" Tricia exclaimed. "A man who cooks!"

"Don't get overexcited," Cornelius replied. "I never said I was good at it."

He was.

Tricia let out a muffled squeal, as if she'd covered her own mouth yet couldn't help herself. "Okay, I'll let you go, then. See you tonight, Dennis."

The phone disconnected, blaring its familiar tone when Tricia was gone.

Cornelius sat in an easy chair positioned for the best view of the beach out back. He kicked his feet up and raised his hands, lacing his fingers behind his head.

At times like these, he wished he had a dog to talk to. He'd even settle for his daughter Hazel's barn cats, Crook and Chase. They were ornery things, but they'd be happy to lend an ear.

It was silly, but in that moment, Cornelius decided to invent an imaginary dog to talk to. One like the black lab he'd seen passing by on the beach. He promised himself that if he made it out of this mess alive, he'd get the puppy, for real. Sully, he'd call him. The name came to mind immediately, and it seemed to fit. Sully would be a loyal companion.

"What do you think, Sully, boy?" he asked out loud. "Should I get to know some people here? I can't go back home. Not yet. Maybe not ever. I'm ready and willing to lay down my life, if it means taking The Cradler's syndicate down. They took my little girl, and they damn near kept her. Now they're targeting other members of my family. They won't stop, until someone stops them. My daughter's pregnant, and I fear they'll be after that baby as well."

He wrung his hands as he stared out at the waves, thinking this through.

"It might be nice to have friendly folks around, if these are my final days," he continued, shrugging his shoulders. "It might also be nice to have people say good things about me after I'm gone, should whatever happens become national news. That's a possibility. I doubt Maureen would have anything positive to say. She'd probably spit on my grave, at this point. Mack Roberts, too. The opportunist prick. He's been waiting for years to get his hands on my wife."

Cornelius could almost hear the fictional Sully whine his agreement.

"It sucks. Badly. I made some mistakes, but I'm not a bad guy. I love my wife," Cornelius explained. "The affair with Linda Peterson was a million years ago. Maureen and I were going through a rough patch, and we were separated at the time. None of the kids know that because we never told them. It took Maureen finding out she was pregnant with Laurel to get us back together. It just so happened that Linda turned up pregnant with Sarah around the same time. How is that so terrible? I thought I was getting a divorce. Linda was—and still is—a beautiful woman. You understand, right, boy?"

Laughing at his own antics, Cornelius stood. He needed a shower and shave, but just a shower would have to do. It would seem suspicious if he showed up clean-shaven to the fish fry. If he was going to interact with the locals beyond a friendly hello here and there, he had better make a plan. That plan began with maintaining his new look. Tricia would need to know him as Dennis with the scraggly beard. There was no other way.

With a few parting words to the imaginary Sully, Cornelius retreated to his bedroom to prepare for the day.

Three

I THOUGHT I smelled a woman's perfume," Laurel mused.

"You can smell that from here?" Brad asked, surprised.

She shrugged. "Due to the pregnancy, I guess. It's one of my new superpowers."

"Speaking of that, isn't your appointment with the OB here in town coming up soon?" he asked.

"It is. How about we focus on whatever that was that sounded like broken glass? Scared me half to death. That isn't good for the baby."

Laurel stopped short of adding that having Jamie in the house wasn't good for Brad, either, but she held her tongue.

"You're right," he said, then gave her a peck on the lips and took the lamp out of her hand. "Let's go see what's going on out there. Jamie probably lost her key. It isn't the first time."

Laurel bristled. She didn't like the thought of Jamie being so comfortable around here. For that matter, she didn't like the thought of Jamie being around here. Period. The woman had been staying with an aunt in Birmingham. What was originally supposed to be for a few days had turned into weeks when the aunt needed someone to take care of her after hip replacement surgery. It had been a welcome reprieve for Laurel. She wished it could have gone on forever. Wasn't Birmingham a nice place to live?

"Are you going out there ... like that?" Laurel asked, gesturing to the bulge in Brad's pants. He was wearing flannel pajama bottoms that left little to the imagination in his current state.

He shrugged. "I can't help what you do to me." Then to Jamie, he called, "be there in a minute!"

Laurel laughed, lightening the mood. "If not for the rude interruption, I might have been able to help you out. If you wanted me to."

He smiled playfully. "Oh, don't tempt me. Because we can make Jamie wait."

"Yeah, but not for long. Plus Jimmy is waiting for an answer, too. I'd say we have important things to tend to this morning. Recreational activities will have to happen later. But I'll be looking forward to tonight."

She leaned over and kissed him passionately on the mouth, a taste of what was to come.

"You keep doing that, and we're not getting out of this room anytime soon," Brad said, glancing down.

Laurel laughed again. "Fine. No more sexy talk."

"Or touch."

"Or touch," she confirmed. "What do you think I should tell Jimmy?"

The mood instantly turned more serious. "I don't know,"

Brad said. "It sounds like he needs you. Are you ready to go back to work?"

"Maybe? Part of me says yes. I can take the lead, and I want to take down whoever did this. I assume Jimmy's most recent find is connected to The Cradler. How could it not be? I can't shake the feeling that The Cradler will continue to up the ante, unless someone intervenes."

"I'm sure you're right about that," Brad replied. "What about the trip to visit your dad? I know you've been angry with him, but do you really want to cancel? We're all packed and ready to go. Mikey will be looking for us in Knoxville in a few hours."

"Would you mind if we cancel?" she asked. "I hate to, but if Jimmy can bring Dad here, then that seems the best course of action—mad at him or not."

"Spoken like someone who is planning to go back to work."

"I'll admit, it feels better to think about working than it does to sit on my hands while people keep secrets from me," she said.

Brad looked stricken, like someone had punched him in the gut. "Don't be mad at me about that, my love. *Please.* Like I told you, I did it for your own good. Your dad made me swear up and down that I wouldn't tell you he was alive. He insisted that it was in your best interest. He didn't want you to become any more of a target."

"Any more?"

Brad had put his foot in his mouth now. "I don't mean that we know you're a target. Because there isn't hard evidence of anything like that. It's just that ... you know ... with the pregnancy and the fact that The Cradler seems to have it out for your family ... I'm saying that we can't be too careful."

"Let's just go," she said simply, nodding to the bedroom door. "We'll talk about this later. After we deal with whatever Jamie's problem is."

Laurel was miffed at the reminder of having been kept in the dark. At the same time, though, she was afraid for herself and her unborn baby. Brad was right—they couldn't be too careful.

"Okay," Brad replied, adjusting his pants. Enough time had passed. He was presentable again.

When they arrived in the living room, Jamie was lounging on the sofa, looking entirely too comfortable. The pose reminded Laurel of a teenager. Her younger siblings had reclined the same way, back in their high school days when they were too full of themselves for their own good.

Laurel wanted to ask Brad how old Jamie was. In the bright overhead light, she suddenly looked at least a decade younger than she had when they'd met out back. Her over-sized peacoat made her look like a child inside its ample fabric.

"Hey," Jamie said, kicking one foot as it dangled a few inches above the hardwood floor.

Lilly sat dutifully nearby, practically smiling. That irked Laurel, too. She had begun to think of Lilly as her own dog.

"Hey, stranger," Brad said. "To what do we owe this pleasure? I thought you were still in Alabama."

Jamie pulled a piece of chewing gum from her pants pocket, carefully opened the silver wrapper, then popped it into her mouth and began to chew. "I was. I rode a Greyhound bus back. It got in at this ungodly hour, and I walked from the station on Main Street. I didn't want to wake you."

"You did," Laurel snapped.

"I didn't know you had company," Jamie said, eying Laurel.

Laurel was growing angry. She remembered Jamie referring to her as a guest when they'd met before. Both terms were passive aggressive, designed to make Laurel feel like the outsider. "I'm not company, you little—"

Brad stopped her by moving to her side and placing a protective arm around her waist, his hand coming to rest on her distended belly. "Jamie, Laurel is my fiancé," he said. "We're having a baby. She is *not* company."

"Or a guest," Laurel added.

Jamie looked pained, but also like she was good at playing games. This was merely one round. "Yes, sir," she said in a phony voice. She winked at Brad and did a little salute. "Whatever you say, sir."

Brad seemed amused. Laurel wanted to gag. She needed to get rid of this pesky woman, and fast. There wasn't room in Brad's life for the both of them.

Satisfied with the introductions, Brad turned his attention to what was, indeed, broken glass. His back door was an apron Dutch style with panes of glass covering the top half. A single pane was broken, the pieces strewn around the floor below. Luckily, Jamie had prevented Lilly from stepping on the jagged pieces and cutting her paws.

"What happened here?" Brad asked.

Jamie blew a bubble with her gum, then popped it unceremoniously. "I tried to use a credit card to wedge in between the door knob and the frame, like you taught me, but it didn't work. The card caught and I jerked, which made the glass break."

"Like you taught her?" Laurel asked.

Brad smirked. "We went over some basic life skills. You know, for a woman on her own in the world. I didn't think she'd use what she knew on me."

"Like I said," Jamie added, "I didn't want to wake you. I knew you kept a key to the carriage house in the kitchen drawer there by the fridge. I thought if I slipped in undetected, I'd get the key and be out before you even realized I was here."

"Did you get cut?" Brad asked, walking toward Jamie with a look of concern on his face.

Laurel rolled her eyes so hard, she thought they might stay stuck that way. "Of course," she said, under her breath.

"A few small scrapes," Jamie said. "Nothing too serious."

Brad sat on the sofa beside her and gingerly lifted her scraped hand to examine it. Jamie shot Laurel a petty look, like a kid who had gotten their way. She might as well have stuck her tongue out and said "na-na, na-na, boo-boo."

Laurel crossed her arms over her chest and rolled her eyes once more, harder this time.

Brad might have spoken the right words when he said that Laurel wasn't company, but his behavior left a lot to be desired. Did he not realize how Jamie was playing him? Was he really so clueless as to be unaware of her intentions? Laurel couldn't help but wonder what had happened between the two of them before she and Brad had reunited here in Appleman's Gap. If she weren't here right now, would Brad be all-in with Jamie? Would they be a couple?

The thought sent a wave of nausea through Laurel's midsection. It had been a while since morning sickness had reared its head, but this scene was enough to bring it right back again in full force.

"Stay here," Brad said, standing. "I have a first aid kit in the bathroom. We'll put some antibiotic ointment on this, along with a few bandages. You'll be fixed up in no time."

Jamie sat up straighter, her fake voice and salute ready. "Thank you, kind sir," she said. "You know how to treat a lady."

Brad smiled, amused. He left the room to fetch the first aid supplies, leaving Laurel and Jamie alone together.

Laurel wasn't sure what came over her all of a sudden, but she had the primal, instinctive desire to assert some dominance over Jamie. She wanted to win a round, too.

"Lilly, come here girl," Laurel called, stooping down to entice the pup.

If Laurel couldn't get Brad under control, perhaps she could command their dog's attention. It was a gamble. Lilly clearly liked Jamie, and for all Laurel knew, Lilly might have ignored her instructions completely. For a tense moment, that's exactly what Laurel thought was happening. Jamie seemed to enjoy it. But Laurel doubled down. Making a kissing sound with her puckered lips, she called Lilly again.

"Come on, girl. Let's go back to bed."

Laurel turned to head for the bedroom. To her delight, she heard Lilly hop down from the sofa, her tags jingling as she followed.

"Good girl," Laurel said, a smug smile covering her face.

Inside the bedroom, Laurel closed the door and climbed back into bed. She couldn't bear to watch Brad apply ointment to Jamie's hand. It was all so scripted. Laurel wouldn't have been surprised to learn that Jamie had broken the glass and created the scene on purpose.

"Good grief," Laurel said to herself. "Ridiculous. All of it."

As if to comfort her, Lilly nuzzled her way to Laurel's arms and made herself soft. Laurel hugged the dog tightly, grateful that she'd decided to follow her back to bed. At least, there was one point in Laurel's favor. Lilly had chosen her.

Ignoring the conversation between Brad and Jamie, Laurel put a pillow over her head and thought about returning to the F.B.I., like Jimmy had asked.

Four

"DAD, IT'S LAUREL."

Cornelius broke into a huge smile when he heard his daughter's voice through the speaker on his mobile phone. She was one of only a handful of people who had his number. She sounded hesitant, which he understood, but she was talking to him. That was a start. He was still wet from the shower, so he threw on a robe and tied it tightly at the waist.

"Laurel, sweetie, how are you? Did you leave yet? You're still coming to see me today, aren't you?"

Using the towel he'd removed from his body, Cornelius ran it over his head a few times to get the excess water off. The motion was more of a nervous one than anything. He had been afraid that Laurel and Mikey would change their minds about visiting. He wouldn't blame them, if they did.

"Laurel, are you still there?" Cornelius asked when she didn't answer right away. He hated feeling like his daughter was a stranger. They had previously been so close.

"I'm here," she replied. "We're still coming."

Cornelius exhaled, the relief washing over him in a blessed feeling of warmth. "Good. I can't wait to see you."

"We can't stay as long as originally planned, though," she said. "I've agreed to go back to work for the F.B.I. Jimmy needs me to take the lead on a case that we suspect is connected to the rest. I'll tell you the details when I get there, but bottom line, we have three days instead of a full week. I promised I'd be back in Tennessee on Wednesday evening. Jimmy has a wedding to go to in Antigua next weekend. It was all I could do to get this much time free. We agreed to split the week down the middle."

"That's okay. I wish we had a full week, but I'll take what I can get," Cornelius said. "I'll just be happy to see you and to hug your neck."

Cornelius didn't sound nearly as Southern as his wife, but every now and then, his phrasing gave his heritage away. Laurel smiled at the expression.

"What time do you think you'll get here?" he asked. "A neighbor lady invited me to a fish fry tonight. I thought you all might want to tag along. If you aren't too tired from traveling, that is."

Laurel found the idea odd. She hadn't realized that her dad was socializing in South Carolina. It made sense. He was only human, after all.

"What's he saying?" Brad asked in the background when Laurel hesitated. "Everything okay?"

"Dad, let me put you on speaker."

"Okay."

A series of rustling sounds could be heard as Laurel hit the speakerphone button and got the phone positioned in the console of Brad's truck. They were driving on Interstate 40 between Appleman's Gap and Knoxville, and the road was becoming curvy as they climbed to a higher elevation.

Laurel hoped Lilly wouldn't get car sick. The pup was beginning to look a little woozy.

"There," Laurel said when the phone was set. "Dad wants us to go to a fish fry tonight. Some neighbor lady invited him."

Laurel had barely escaped the morning's encounter with Jamie unscathed. The last thing she wanted to witness was a random woman flirting with her dad under the guise of welcoming him to the neighborhood. Maureen might have been distracted by Mack Roberts for the time being, but Laurel hadn't given up on the idea of her parents getting back together.

"Sounds fun," Brad said. "I'm in. If you aren't too tired, babe. Maybe you can nap on the ride down."

"Maybe."

"Is that a yes?" Cornelius asked tentatively. He wasn't sure how his daughter was feeling at this point in her pregnancy, and he didn't want to push her.

"Sure," Laurel replied. "I imagine Mikey will be fine with it. Any chance to drink a beer and sit on the beach is good with him."

"Great!" Cornelius said, perhaps sounding a little too excited. He couldn't help himself. "I'm supposed to bring hush puppies. I'd better go to the store and gather the supplies. Can I get you anything? Something to eat while you're here at the house?"

He knew their favorites, but thought he'd ask, anyway. He figured Laurel might have cravings that meant she'd want something new.

"Some fresh fruits and vegetables would be good," she replied.

"Brad?" Cornelius asked.

"I can eat anything. You know that."

They all laughed. It was true. Brad was an enthusiastic eater, and he wasn't picky.

They ended the call, promising to keep in close touch along the way so Cornelius could keep track of their progress.

"Well, that was somewhat awkward, wasn't it, Sully?" Cornelius said to his imaginary dog after the call disconnected. He was really going for it when it came to carrying on a conversation with his future, hypothetical pooch. "I hope the visit turns out to be more relaxed than that phone call was. Maybe having Mikey in the mix will loosen things up. Bummer that they have to leave early. I'll need to cull my list of activities. I was planning to hit all of the tourist hotspots."

Shrugging, he opened the plantation-style doors to the master bedroom closet and selected an outfit for the day. He'd wear shorts and a t-shirt while he ran errands, then would change into something more beachy chic for the gathering tonight. He wondered what Tricia looked like. He hoped she was as pretty as her voice made her sound.

He had just buttoned his Army green cargo shorts and slid a South Carolina Aquarium t-shirt over his head when his mobile phone rang again.

"Mr. Paulson, what can I do for you?" he asked. "Let me guess. There's a new development that seems connected to what we're working on and you need my daughter home on Wednesday night to handle it."

"Is this a secure line?" Jimmy asked, skipping the formalities.

Cornelius paused, sensing the seriousness. "Semi-secure. Do you need it completely secure?"

"Yes."

"Give me thirty minutes. You'll hear from me then."

Moving quickly, Cornelius exited his rental home. Careful to keep a grocery list in hand and in plain view should anyone photograph him, he climbed into his Lexus sedan and slowly backed out of the driveway. The sensible sedan blended in with other vehicles in the neighborhood. His focus when in public was maintaining a low profile. He didn't want to seem out of the ordinary.

He kept his speed down until he reached Highway 17 in Mount Pleasant so as not to draw attention to himself. Once on the Ravenel Bridge and over open water, he picked up the pace, speeding when possible all the way to the Exxon station across the street from Ye Ole Fashioned Ice Cream on the south side of Charleston.

Pulling a palmetto tree and moon ball cap low over his eyes, Cornelius went inside the gas station and paid cash for two Slim Jims, a bottle of Mountain Dew, and a burner phone. He then headed south on Savannah Highway and made the turn for James Island County Park, where he found an isolated area and trekked into the marshland so he wouldn't be heard.

He took a deep breath, then—using an end-to-end encrypted communication app—dialed Jimmy's number. It had been twenty-nine minutes. He was ahead of schedule.

"Secure line. Go," Cornelius said when Jimmy picked up.

"I respect you too much to mince words," Jimmy said. "Besides, we should make this quick."

"Ten-four. Go ahead."

"We've got a serious problem," Jimmy began. "An old informant, who was previously under protective custody, is not any longer. Word at the Bureau is that he has decided to go public. This informant has documents and testimonies linking you to The Cradler's operations. He thinks he's doing the right thing by exposing you. He's threatening to go to the media."

"What kind of evidence does he have?" Cornelius asked, squinting against the sun that was climbing higher in the sky.

Jimmy sighed. "The informant claims to have transaction records and communications that suggest you were involved with The Cradler's syndicate."

"So? I'm a dead man, remember? Who is going to care?"

"Yeah, well, his threat to go public puts you and the entire investigation at risk. This guy says he can prove that you were in deep with The Cradler's crew. If he goes to the media, your cover is blown. Your fake death would have been for nothing. No one wants that, least of all your pregnant daughter. From what I can tell, you're on thin ice with her as it is."

"You aren't wrong. Then how about you tell the informant that I was working undercover? Since I'm supposed to be dead, that might be okay, right?"

Jimmy sighed. "We can't do that, my friend. You've risked far too much and chased The Cradler for far too long to let your cover be blown by some hothead who thinks he's a hero. If word gets out that you were working undercover, it suddenly becomes plausible that you still are. I won't take that chance. You and your entire family would be in danger."

Cornelius stayed quiet for a moment, thinking. "I must know this informant. If he knows so much about me, he must be someone I worked with. A former employee of my department?"

"I can't reveal his identity. You understand how this works."

Cornelius found a bench, then walked over and sat down with his elbows on his knees. A beautiful blue heron landed in the marshland in front of him. The graceful bird spread its wings, as if to offer support.

"What do you want me to do?" Cornelius asked.

"As of right now, hell if I know," Jimmy replied. "I'll update you if the situation develops. But keep your eyes and ears open. Be ready for anything."

<h1 style="text-align:center">Five</h1>

"THERE HE IS," Brad said with a grin as Mikey threw his duffel bag in the backseat of Brad's truck and then climbed in after it. Lilly wagged her tail as she moved over to make room. A messenger bag draped over one shoulder was the only other piece of luggage Mikey carried.

"Mr. America?" Mikey asked with a laugh.

"Hey, whatever floats your boat," Brad said. "I see you packed light. Will that get you through four days at the beach?"

"Four days?" Mikey asked. "I thought we were staying a week."

"You can if you want, little brother," Laurel replied, "but I have to be back in Appleman's Gap on Wednesday night for work. Brad, Lilly, and I will leave South Carolina that morning."

"Work ... at the F.B.I.?"

"Jimmy practically begged, so yes," Laurel explained. "A woman's mutilated body was found in Cedar Hollow. They think a baby was cut out of her womb. Samira and Malik aren't experienced enough to lead the investigation, so I couldn't very well say no."

"Oh, wow," Mikey said. "That's so sad. Did they identify her yet?"

Laurel shook her head. "No. The body was just found last night. I heard about it early this morning. Jimmy is flying down from D.C. to handle things until I get back."

Mikey nodded his understanding. "No worries. Duty calls. You tell Dad yet?"

The morning sun shone on the dewy grass as they followed the winding road out of Mikey's Knoxville neighborhood and turned east onto Cumberland Avenue. They'd get back on the Interstate just before reaching the University of Tennessee campus. Classes had recently resumed for the spring semester. Even though it was a Saturday, the campus was likely to be busy.

"I did. Talked to him when we were passing through Harriman a little while ago. He seemed disappointed, but okay with it," Laurel said. "What could he say, really?"

"Yeah," Mikey replied. He was tall enough that he had to move his knees to one side to fit comfortably in the back seat of Brad's truck. He shifted in his seat as he got settled.

"Hey, man," Brad said, handing a plastic bag from a travel store to Mikey. "We picked up some snacks. There are power bars, trail mix, and a couple of bananas in there. Bottles of water are on the floorboard behind my seat."

"I see that my sister influenced your selections," Mikey replied, grinning. "Gone are the days of donuts and soda, huh?"

Brad shrugged, then shot Mikey a knowing glance.

"You'll thank me when our baby doesn't come out with two heads," Laurel replied.

"If it's a boy, he ought to," Brad quipped.

Laurel opened her eyes wide in mock surprise. She wasn't actually surprised, though. She was well aware of how Brad's mind worked. Weren't all men that way?

"Stop it," she said, swatting him playfully on the arm. "You know what I meant."

Mikey shook his head and laughed. "You two crack me up," he mused.

Turning back to face the front and pulling a knee to her chest, Laurel said, "You might not have been laughing earlier this morning."

Brad tensed. His expression seemed to say that he'd like to talk about anything but Jamie Beck. Yet, here they were, trapped in the truck together for another six or seven hours, depending on traffic. If Laurel had grievances to air, she had plenty of time and presumably, a sympathetic ear in Mikey.

"Here we go," Brad said.

"What?" Laurel asked, the mood shifting. "Can't I tell my own brother about my problems?"

Mikey mumbled an "uh oh" under his breath, then stroked Lilly's head for support.

"I'm not sure I'd call her a *problem*," Brad said. "What's so bad about her? She's a nice person."

"Who are we talking about?" Mikey asked.

"Jamie," Laurel and Brad replied, in unison, one's tone more contentious than the other's.

"I see."

"She broke into our house this morning," Laurel said, "and she makes goo-goo eyes at Brad every chance she gets."

"Come on, now, that's not true," Brad replied. "I don't see her like that. Laurel Dane, you are the love of my life. I've said it again and again."

Laurel scoffed. She wasn't dismissing Brad's statement, but she wasn't entirely convinced, either. "You've told me, but Jamie didn't get the memo. You seem to enjoy her attention."

Brad glanced at Mikey in the rearview mirror. The two of them were privy to an important detail that Laurel didn't know. The secrets were becoming too much, yet Brad had promised he wouldn't tell his fiance this particular tidbit until a later date.

"Listen, Sis," Mikey began, "even strangers can see that Brad is completely devoted to you. I'm sure Jamie sees that, too. Go easy on my guy."

"Thanks, Mikey," Brad said.

"Your guy?" Laurel asked, turning to look at her brother.

"I told you, I've been rooting for him the whole time. When you were broken up, it was all I could do to hold my tongue and wait for you to come to your senses. Brad is a good, honest dude. You've got nothing to worry about there."

"I appreciate that," Brad replied. "Sounds like I need someone on my side."

"Okay, then," Laurel said, crossing her arms over her chest defensively. The pose was more difficult now with her growing belly. "Why does she have to live with us? Kick her out. Let her find her own place, preferably in another city. I don't even want to see her around Appleman's Gap."

"What do you have against her?" Brad asked as he set his cruise control and settled in for the drive through the mountains. They'd stop for a bathroom break—and maybe some lunch—across the North Carolina line in Asheville.

"She's immature, for one," Laurel said. "How old is she, anyway? Seventeen?"

"She's twenty-three."

"Way too young for you."

"Good thing I'm not interested in her, then," Brad replied.

"Yeah, but were you?" Laurel asked. "When we were broken up? Did you two sleep together?"

Brad glanced at Mikey in the mirror again. Mikey shook his head and raised his hands in the air, letting Brad know that he was on his own.

"Would it matter if we did?" Brad asked slowly. His tone was calculated. Cautious. "You and I were broken up. You told me to go and live my life. You said you didn't want to be with me. You even turned down my marriage proposal. I have to admit, that really hurt."

"I'm not hearing a no," Laurel said sadly.

The news wasn't a revelation. She'd been able to tell the moment she'd met Jamie. She hated it, though. She hadn't been romantically involved with anyone during the time she and Brad were broken up. Of course, she'd known she was pregnant. Brad hadn't had the benefit of that knowledge until they'd reunited in Appleman's Gap, after the carjacking.

"Babe, don't sound so sad," Brad said, reaching out for her hand. She let him take it, reluctantly. "You are my one and only. I swear on everything that's holy. It's you and only you, until my dying day. Hell, beyond my dying day ... if there is a beyond. It's you."

A single tear ran down Laurel's cheek. She quickly wiped

it away, then turned to look out the side window. Sensing that she needed comfort, Lilly put her front paws on the center console and nuzzled against Laurel's elbow. She woofed, asking if she could move to the front and sit on Laurel's lap.

Laurel nodded. "Come on up here, sweet girl."

She had to let go of Brad's hand to make room for the dog. He kept his hand nearby, at the ready in case she wanted it again. Meanwhile, Mikey leaned forward and gave his sister's shoulder a reassuring squeeze.

"We all love you, Sis," Mikey said. "Lots of people do."

She took a deep, cleansing breath as Lilly leaned into her. "I know. I'm sorry to get emotional like this. I just don't understand why the girl—or young woman or whatever—has to live with us."

"She lives in the carriage house," Brad clarified. "Not *with* us."

"Close enough, and too close for comfort."

Brad could see goosebumps form on Laurel's arms, so he turned the dial to add heat to her side of the cab. "Because I made a promise. That's why. I need you to trust me."

"A promise? How about your promise to me? I didn't envision a twenty three year-old hussy being a third wheel in our relationship. I certainly didn't envision someone hanging around with us once the baby arrives. Our little family needs privacy to grow and flourish."

"She'll be gone by then," Mikey said, sounding a little too sure.

"How do you know?" Laurel asked, whipping her head around to see him.

"Because I know. Just trust me," Mikey replied.

"Oh, great," Laurel said, waving a hand in the air. "Now I'm supposed to trust both of you?"

"Yes," they said.

"Please, babe."

Before she could protest and ask more questions, Laurel's phone rang. She picked it up out of the center console, seeing Kanesha's name on the screen.

"It's Kanesha," she said. "I wonder what she wants. She knew I was going out of town."

The women had become friends, talking and meeting at least once each week to catch up.

"Answer it," Brad said. "Might be something important."

Laurel nodded. "Hello?"

Kanesha's voice was frantic. It was obvious that she had been crying. She spoke so fast that Laurel could barely understand a word that she said. Something about a sister and brother-in-law who were visiting from South Florida.

"Kanesha, honey, slow down," Laurel said. "I can't understand you. Is this about your sister? Tiana is her name, right?"

Laurel put a finger in one ear to help her hear better out of the other one. Concerned, Brad turned the fan down on the heat and made sure Lilly would sit still and quiet.

"My sister is eight months pregnant," Kanesha said slowly. "She never came home last night. Laurel, she's missing."

Six

CORNELIUS CRACKED the SIM card and tossed it and the burner phone into the marsh. The heron didn't fly away, but instead looked on, seeming amused.

"Well, damn," he said. "This complicates matters. Be ready for anything, huh?"

He thought about how, if Sully were here, the dog would sympathize with him. He'd probably jump into the marsh and chase the bird away, making a ruckus as he went. Sully would need a bath after that, too, but Cornelius wouldn't mind. Seeing the dog's joy at life's simple pleasures would be worth it.

One day.

For now, Cornelius would have to make due with a visit from his daughter's dog, Lilly. He hadn't met the pup yet, but she sounded darling. Lilly would get him his dog fix for a while. That reminded him, he had better pick up some treats for her at the store. Laurel and Brad were bringing her food with them, but Cornelius knew that any good dog grandpa should have treats on hand for the first visit.

Figuring there was no use crying over spilled milk, Cornelius dusted himself off and returned to his sedan. There were hushpuppies to be made, after all. It would potentially arouse more suspicion if he bowed out of the fish fry. It was important that he move forward. Business as usual. He started the engine and slowly pulled out of the parking lot, even though what he really wanted to do was to sit a while longer and enjoy the scenery.

At a much more relaxed pace than the drive down, the former policeman followed his path back to the main drag on U.S. 17, around the marina and past the Medical University of South Carolina, and over the Ravenel Bridge as he headed north. He stopped at a grocery store in Mount Pleasant, just a few miles inland from his rental house on Sullivan's Island. He doubted he'd run into anyone who'd recognize him, but "Dennis" might as well get friendly. He'd been spending far too long holed up at home. For his own sanity and for the potential need to have witnesses who could insist that he was a regular Joe, Cornelius was ready to show his scruffily-bearded face. The news about the informant only made him more eager to implement his plan. Hiding in plain sight was harder than it sounded. There was a method to the madness. It was time to pay more attention to that method.

The Piggly Wiggly was crowded when he arrived. Shoppers in casual clothes filled the parking lot, hurrying in and out with that particular weekend frenzy that ensues when people have enough free time to shop, but there are other things they want to move on to when their chores are done.

Good, he thought as he walked through the sliding glass doors, careful to turn his head to one side at precisely the right time so as to confuse any facial recognition systems that might scan footage from the security cameras. The ballcap helped, too.

"Welcome in, sir," a young man in a red apron said cheerfully. "Can I help you find anything?"

"Got my list in hand," Cornelius replied, holding the handwritten paper up as proof. He took a metal cart from the corral and placed the list carefully in the basket.

He walked past the customer service desk, scanning the row of employees perched behind their registers. He intended to target one whom he'd make up an excuse to chat with. Then he'd return to the store again and again, until he was considered a regular.

Right off the bat, he spotted three potential cashiers who looked friendly. He moved on toward the produce section, deciding that he'd make a choice between the three when his cart was full and he was ready to check out. All three were women, a fact that made him chuckle.

Cornelius Dane had a weakness for women. He was becoming more and more aware of it as he aged. Or maybe he had been working overtime to delude himself about his ... *tendencies* ... when he'd been married to Maureen. Of course, he still was married to her, technically. It was complicated. Shrugging, he pushed those thoughts aside and got busy looking for fresh okra.

He was examining green okra pods when he felt a metal bar ram him in the back of one leg. He immediately recognized it as another shopping cart that someone had brought too close. It hurt like the dickens.

"Ouch!" Cornelius exclaimed, reaching down to touch the injured area. It felt like some skin had come off. That was going to be sore later.

"Braxton! I told you to be careful, son. Slow down," a woman shouted as she wrestled the offending cart away from a young boy with sandy blonde hair and a gap where his two front teeth should have been.

The woman was attractive. She was fit and trim, and she was dressed in form-fitting athletic clothing as if she'd just come from an exercise class. Cornelius thought probably one of those fancy barre or pilates classes, by the looks of her. Her thick, chestnut-brown hair bounced against her shoulders. He couldn't help but notice that the ring finger on her left hand had no ring. Not even a suntan mark where a ring used to be.

Gathering himself, he sprang into action.

"No worries, ma'am," he said in his best flirty tone. "It's just a little scrape. It happens. Braxton didn't mean to bump me, I'm sure."

"Ram" was a better description than "bump," but who was asking?

"He gets overexcited at times," the woman said bashfully, her body language responding to Cornelius' tone. She was interested. That much was clear.

There was a moment of awkward silence as they sized each other up.

"I'm Dennis. Dennis McCready," Cornelius said, extending his hand to shake hers.

"Carmen Bullock," she replied, taking his hand. "And this is my son, Braxton."

Her hand was warm and smooth. Cornelius enjoyed her touch. It had been too long since he'd felt a woman's soft skin.

"Forgive me for being forward," he said, "but is there a

Mr. Bullock? Should I be concerned that a tough guy will come around the corner and tell me I shouldn't be flirting with his beautiful wife?"

Carmen blushed, then smiled and shook her head. "No such tough guy. Braxton's dad … isn't in the picture. Bullock is my maiden name."

Cornelius raised his brows, a sly smile spreading across his lips. He loved this part of the cat and mouse game that was male-female dating. He knew how to play it, and he enjoyed the sport.

He gazed at Carmen with admiration, waiting for her to make the next move. He took a long, slow glance down her figure, feasting his eyes on her tight-fitting yoga pants and the way they clung to her muscular thighs.

"What are you going to do with that okra, Dennis McCready?" she asked.

Braxton became occupied with a display of animal cracker boxes on an endcap nearby. Carmen kept a watchful eye, but she let him explore so that her focus could remain with Cornelius.

"I'm going to cook it," he said simply.

He smiled and adjusted the ballcap on his head. Even as a man who had recently turned seventy, Cornelius was a handsome devil. The ladies liked him just as much as he adored them. Apparently, the scruffy beard wasn't slowing him down.

"Who taught you how to do that?"

"My momma, a long, long time ago," he replied. "Is there something you're trying to say about that?" He put a gentle hand on her wrist, lacing his thumb and index finger around her petite bones. "What? Can't men cook? I'd like to cook for you. I know how to please a woman. I think you'd be impressed with my skills ... in the kitchen and ... elsewhere."

Cornelius chuckled, imagining the old Austin Powers character played by Mike Myers telling him to behave as Carmen turned darker shades of pink and red.

If he had to guess, Cornelius would put Carmen in her twenties. Maybe early thirties, but that was less likely. She'd probably gotten pregnant with Braxton young. Apparently, she was raising the boy on her own. She might like an older, experienced man to treat her right and show her what it felt like to be admired and cherished.

"Can I take you out sometime?" Cornelius asked. "I'm new in town and would love for you to show me around. I'm staying out on Sullivan's Island. Right on the beach."

Carmen smiled at that.

"Are you from here?" he asked.

She nodded. "Born and raised in Mount Pleasant. Graduated from Wando High School, just down the road from here. I could show you around."

"Good, then it's a date," he said. "How about tomorrow night? I'll pick you up at seven?"

"Okay."

He nodded, then tore a piece from the bottom of his grocery list and wrote down his name and number. "Call me," he said.

"Will do," she replied, just as Braxton came barreling back, having grown bored with the animal crackers. "I'll get a babysitter."

They parted ways with a lingering look that promised more.

"Well, well, well, Sully, boy," Cornelius said to his imaginary dog once Carmen was out of sight. "Daddy's got a real date. So much for needing to make friends with a cashier. I did one even better."

Cornelius grinned to himself, then finished his shopping. Carmen would be waiting for him tomorrow. Tonight, he had Tricia to impress. Plus, of course, his family.

No pressure.

Seven

THE DRIVE through the mountains and down I-26 to Charleston was uneventful for Laurel, Brad, Mikey, and Lilly, except for the fact that Laurel had a sinking feeling about Kanesha's sister.

Appleman's Gap was a small town. Hearing that Tiana was pregnant and had gone missing around the same time that a mutilated body was found did not bode well for the woman's safety—or her baby's. Jimmy was on a plane from D.C. to Nashville, so Laurel hadn't been able to reach him by phone. She'd reached out to Samira and Malik for an update on the case, but since Laurel wasn't officially part of the investigation yet and had not been briefed, they weren't allowed to tell her anything.

Brad had inquired with his officers and was waiting on a call back. Not that he expected them to know much. Jimmy had been clear that local police were not involved with the murder investigation.

It was heartbreaking to everyone involved. The Cradler was terrorizing their beloved little town, making people afraid to leave their homes. Someone needed to stop him, and fast. Otherwise, he'd keep kidnapping and killing innocent mothers and babies. Laurel was glad that she'd agreed to go back to work for the F.B.I. on the case. Nothing felt worse than wanting to help and not being able to. This way, she could, hopefully, make a difference. She'd love to take The Cradler down and get his goons off the streets. Every single one of them deserved to be behind bars.

"Babe, what are you thinking about?" Brad asked as they crossed the Ravenel Bridge and approached Mount Pleasant.

It was mid-afternoon. While they had made good time, the light was beginning to fade, thanks to an early sunset that time of year. Laurel wondered if there would be lights on the beach for the fish fry. Surely, there would.

"Mostly The Cradler," she said. "After all these years with the Bureau, I still don't understand what is wrong with people. It's remarkable to me that someone like The Cradler can operate such a sophisticated criminal enterprise. Like, who teaches these assholes the necessary skills, you know?"

Mikey chuckled from the backseat. "Fair point."

"In The Cradler's case, he learned from his dad," Brad said. "This guy is simply continuing the family tradition. Some family that is. Wasn't the father the one in charge when … when your dad first began tracking them?"

He was careful not to mention Laurel's kidnapping as a child. She hadn't fully remembered what had happened. It was a touchy subject.

She nodded. "That's right. The father didn't have a creepy villain name like The Cradler, as far as I know. He went by his real name—Lucian Somerset—which isn't even a bad name. Somerset sounds kind of cheery, doesn't it?"

"I agree," Brad replied. "The Cradler sure took things up a notch when he decided to call himself that. It sounds menacing."

"Definitely creepy," Mikey added.

"Lucian is dead and buried now," Laurel continued. "Died of a vicious attack by other inmates while serving life in prison at Riverbend Maximum Security Institution. I guess even hardened criminals don't like it when you mess with kids."

Brad and Mikey both nodded their approval.

"Damn straight," Mikey said.

Brad eyed Laurel, well aware that she was thinking about more than just that. She'd been in law enforcement long enough to know there weren't answers to those types of questions. Sometimes, though, it was easier to wonder about criminal motivations than it was to admit that you were afraid.

"Are you worried about Sarah and Jasper?" he asked softly.

Laurel sighed, then nodded. "I am. I don't know if we'll ever be friends again, but I love them. I don't want anything to happen to them."

"I promise, my officers are on top of it," Brad replied. "Two are stationed outside their house to monitor for suspicious activity. Plus, we have security cameras and alarms to monitor and alert us to any unauthorized access or movements. And if there's even the slightest indication that The Cradler's coming after them again, we'll move the family to a safe house where they can stay until the threat is neutralized."

"Sounds thorough," Mikey said.

"I know," Laurel replied. "I still worry. Now I have to add

Kanesha's sister to the list. I don't have a good feeling about that."

What she didn't mention, but they all knew, was that she worried for herself and her unborn baby, too. It was a nice reprieve to be in South Carolina for a few days, but Appleman's Gap was her home. Her mind and heart remained there, no matter how far she traveled. In fact, Laurel and Brad still needed to make some decisions about their future. More and more as time went on, Laurel saw that future as being in her hometown of Appleman's Gap. Washington, D.C. had been home for a while, but she wanted to raise her baby in a quieter place, around family.

Lilly whined, signaling her need for a potty break. Laurel and Brad looked at each other.

"Should we stop?" Laurel asked. "We're less than fifteen minutes from Dad's rental house, but the poor pup has to go. It's been almost three hours since she was out."

Brad chuckled. "Sure. Let's stop. I suppose this is good practice for having a baby. No way will we be able to drive for three hours straight without stopping once our little one comes along."

"Well, maybe," Mikey said, as a seasoned father of three. "But usually, you have to drive overnight to get that much in one stretch. We did it once on the way to Disney in Orlando. The drive was peaceful, but keeping up with the kids the next day when they were all amped up and Jess and I were exhausted was brutal. So, yeah. Just plan to stop."

As they reached the base of the bridge, Brad pulled into the Mount Pleasant Memorial Waterfront Park and eased the truck to a stop.

"You remembered," Laurel said.

"How could I forget? We had one of the best weekends here," he replied, leaning over and kissing her. "I remember seeing dogs at the park when we sat on the benches looking at the water. That's when we first talked about getting a dog of our own."

Mikey balked, then tossed an empty plastic bottle at them. "Oh, please. Get a room, you two."

They all laughed together, then Brad hooked Lilly's leash to her collar and stepped out of the truck. Laurel and Mikey followed, everyone appreciating the warmer temperatures as compared to back home in Tennessee.

"This is glorious," Mikey said, stretching and breathing in the salty air as they took in the panoramic views of Charleston Harbor. The USS Yorktown was visible in the distance. "I see why Dad likes it here. It's January, and I don't even need a jacket."

"You've never been here before?" Brad asked.

"Nope. First time. But I think it's safe to say it won't be my last. Jess and the kids would love it."

"I'm sure they would," Brad said. "Maybe Laurel and I could get married here, then everyone would have an excuse to come down and celebrate with us.

Laurel grabbed her handbag out of the truck, then Brad locked the doors as they headed for the bathroom pavilion and the dog relief area. She didn't react to his comment about the wedding. That was another thing they really needed to discuss and get some plans in place. She felt almost ready. Jamie still bothered her, though, and she'd need to reach a better frame of mind with regard to the troublesome woman before she'd move forward with wedding planning.

"I'll walk Lilly, then meet you back," Brad said, sensing Laurel's discomfort and deciding not to push.

Lilly pulled eagerly at the end of her leash and panted. It was the dog equivalent of crossing her legs and hopping up and down. She was desperate.

"I'm making a beeline to the bathroom," Laurel said. "As if anyone's surprised. This baby is pressing on my bladder."

They laughed. Laurel was really showing now. Her bump could be hidden if she wore a big sweater or coat, but she'd peeled all of that off as they'd neared the coast. The form-fitting top she was wearing didn't leave much to the imagination.

"I'll hit the bathrooms, too," Mikey said. "Although, no baby is pressing on my bladder."

"Thanks for clarifying that, man," Brad joked.

Mikey lifted his shirt and forced his stomach forward in his best beer-belly pose, but his toned abs didn't offer much to work with.

They split up, all having a good time and bustling with the energy of the scenic coastal locale. It was going to be a great trip.

Things took a turn for the worse, however, the moment that Laurel opened the door to the bathroom and stepped inside. A strange woman was there, crouched oddly at the end of a row of sinks. Her eyes were wild, like she was either mentally ill ... or drugged. Laurel looked directly at her, smiled confidently, then said hello.

Laurel's instincts told her to turn around and walk out, but she really needed to relieve herself, so she let her logical mind override her instincts. That was a mistake.

She stepped into the stall closest to the entrance, pulled

her pants down, and did her business. As she was cleaning up and preparing to stand, she saw a long shadow approaching. Whoever it belonged to, they were much bigger than the woman she'd seen. They were also approaching from the other direction. A pair of feet wearing black work boots came to a stop near her.

Thinking quickly, Laurel realized that her phone was in her handbag. It was hanging on a hook high above her, and there were two different zippers between her and the phone. She wouldn't be able to reach it without standing. Even then, she'd have to fumble with the zippers before she could get it out. She mentally kicked herself for not holding the phone in her hand. Of course, she should have left the bathroom the minute she felt uneasy. Wetting her pants would have been a better option.

She'd seen countless cases during her time at the Bureau—assaults, kidnappings, and even murders—where the victim had an instinct to flee, but didn't. She'd also talked to witnesses who had listened to their guts and lived to tell about it. The data was clear. Humans are the only animals who let their logical minds override what the lizard brain knows. They fare poorly when they do. They tell themselves that it will probably be fine, or that they shouldn't judge people without getting to know them. Nope. All wrong.

"Hello?" Laurel called out in her best Agent Dane voice. She'd been taught to sound commanding and in control. "Is there something I can do for you?"

As an agent, she was trained to be aware of her surroundings at all times. That included identifying potential threats, knowing exits, and recognizing anything unusual. She had been doing that ... mostly. Not well enough, though, as she'd be the first to admit. After the carjacking a few months prior, Laurel had vowed to be more careful. Was she slipping?

She heard a man breathing heavily, then someone—presumably the woman she saw—scurried out behind him. Was this a tag-team situation? Had the woman somehow signaled that she'd caught one and that the man should come in to close the deal?

Laurel thought through what she remembered about the crowd outside and the likely distance to Brad and Mikey. They'd be able to come to her aid faster than any local police. They'd also be personally invested in doing what was necessary to keep her and the baby safe. She wondered if they'd hear her, should she yell in her loudest voice. She wasn't sure.

She didn't have a weapon on her. Truth be told, she'd found herself shying away from firearms since she'd learned she was pregnant. Brad had a gun in his truck. She didn't know if he had it on his person or not.

Regardless of what she should have done a few minutes prior, it was time to assess the risk in the here and now. Laurel thought back to her training. She had to assess the level of threat and determine the best course of action, whether to confront, evade, or call for backup. She'd already confronted the man by calling out to him, so she decided to continue with that path. If she could get out of the bathroom, she'd likely be able to make it to Brad or Mikey safely.

Her task was to get herself out the door, and to work on accessing her phone and calling Brad as she went. She told herself she could do this. If all else failed, she'd scream the word fire as loud as she could. It had been proven that people would respond to a call for fire more reliably than they would a call for help.

Laurel stood, fastening the button on her pants and grabbing for the keys that were in an outside pocket of her handbag. She positioned three keys between the fingers of her right hand then made a tight fist, creating a makeshift weapon. Then she began digging for her phone.

"I'm coming out there, and I'm armed," she said loudly, her voice strong and clear. "Back off!"

Her mind raced, remembering the day of the carjacking with Baby Jasper, the day her dad had someone grab her in the parking lot of Leopold's so that he could reveal himself as still alive, and the time she was kidnapped as a child. Terror coursed through every inch of her body. It didn't matter that as an F.B.I. agent Laurel had received extensive training to handle a variety of scenarios, including being attacked in public while off duty. She was afraid for herself and her baby. She'd been traumatized one too many times, and she wasn't over it yet.

Suddenly, the man stepped closer, closing the gap between himself and the door to the stall that provided a modicum of protection for Laurel and her unborn child. Laurel held her breath, waiting to see what he might do. She felt for her phone frantically, but it had fallen down to the bottom of her handbag. If she yelled for Brad and Mikey, it would show weakness. She didn't want to do that unless she was out of other options.

Before she could make a decision about her next step, she felt a crushing blow come crashing down on her head. Within seconds, everything went black. The last thing she remembered was sliding to the floor, cradling her distended belly in one hand in an effort to protect it.

Eight

GREASE BUBBLED in the fryer as Cornelius' hushpuppies cooked to a golden brown. He'd considered making a healthier version in an air fryer, but decided he shouldn't mess with a Lowcountry tradition when he was just getting to know new folks. The okra was already done—cut, seasoned, and fried to perfection.

Cornelius had gone out of his way to visit a vineyard in Wadmalaw Island that afternoon after he'd dropped his groceries off at the house. He'd picked up some red wine and a simple mead, figuring that both would pair well with fish.

He'd been a mead guy for a long time, even making and bottling it at home in Appleman's Gap. Something about the old world charm of the honey wine tickled his fancy. He figured Maureen had probably thrown out all of his fermenting supplies by now. That was a shame. At least, he could still partake in a good mead from the local vineyard. Hopefully, he'd have a chance to make his own again some-day. Maybe an apple mead that could be sold at the orchard. They were long overdue for a new product.

He glanced at the old-fashioned clock on the wall, its hands ticking away. It was almost time to meet Tricia at the lighthouse for the fish fry. Cornelius had expected Laurel, Mikey, and Brad to be there by now. He ran a hand over his beard as he thought about whether or not to wait. He could warm the okra and hushpuppies in the oven for a while, but they'd get soggy if he didn't deliver them soon.

"Should we wait, Sully?" he asked his imaginary dog. "There's a pretty lady at a fish fry who will be looking for me any time now. I wouldn't want to disappoint her, would I?"

Cornelius had done some internet research on Ms. Tricia Bowers. If her social media pictures were accurate representations of her looks, she was every bit as attractive as he'd hoped. His skin pinked just thinking about it.

He sent a quick text to Laurel, explaining where he'd be. She could meet him there.

He was already dressed for the event, so he packed the food and wine bottles into a large insulated bag, then locked up and headed out the back door to the beach. The lighthouse was a short walk from his rental home. No need to drive.

As he strolled along the beach, water gently lapping over his feet, he reflected on how nice it was to take a break from his responsibilities. Not to mention, it was a welcomed relief to hang out with other people.

Cornelius had spent so much time alone over the past few months since he'd faked his death and gone deep undercover. He was a natural extrovert, too, and all the alone time had taken a toll. Having his kids come to visit and accepting Tricia's invitation to the fish fry had awakened something in him. Meeting Carmen had stoked those fires further. Things were looking up.

As he neared the lighthouse and saw the crowd gathered under string lights on the beach nearby, Jimmy's words of warning echoed in his mind. Jimmy had said to be ready for anything. Cornelius would be vigilant, but he was also going to let loose and have a little fun. A man can only work so long and hard before he needs a break. No one would fault him for that.

Faces came into view, and Cornelius immediately spotted Tricia's.

"Hello, there, pretty lady," he said with a grin. "If I didn't know better, I'd think you were standing here waiting for me."

She smiled, dipping one shoulder and lifting one foot in a flirty pose. Her long, blonde hair was tied back, showcasing her elegant neck and strong jawline. A flowing dress hugged her curves and accentuated her ample bust. For a woman in her fifties—according to her social media profiles—Tricia was a stone-cold fox. She could give Carmen a run for her money any day. And that was saying something.

Cornelius felt like he had won some sort of lottery. Not one, but two beautiful women were interested in him.

"I might have been waiting for you, Dennis," Tricia said as she stepped forward and gave him a lingering kiss on the cheek. Her hand rested on his chest as she did, sending plea-surable sensations throughout his body. He thought again about how long it had been since he'd felt a woman's touch. Too long, that was for sure.

"Is it the hushpuppies you can't live without?" he joked.

"I have them right here in the bag. Okra, too. No need to get all hot and bothered."

"It isn't just the hushpuppies."

Remembering Tricia's rapid speech on the phone, Cornelius was surprised by how calm and smooth she was now. "You don't even seem nervous," he said.

"Are you ... nervous?" she asked as she turned and gave his bottom a squeeze.

Cornelius jumped, startled by her forwardness.

Seeing him caught off guard, Tricia fumbled her words, reverting back to the fast-talking, flighty personality he'd heard on the phone.

"I'm sorry. I don't know what I was thinking. How rude of me. I guess I got carried away. It's dusk and the lights are so pretty and you look so good, oh, and you smell so good, too—"

"No worries," he said. "It's fine. You just threw me off there for a minute. I didn't expect you to be so aggressive."

She lowered her head, smiling with both her mouth and her eyes. "Do you ... *like* ... me being aggressive?"

Aiming to match her energy, he wrapped his free hand quickly around her trim waist and pulled her to him. When she came to rest, their lips were inches apart. He could feel the heat from her body. "I do."

Cornelius' shorts suddenly felt a few sizes too tight, and he thought seriously about inviting Tricia to a darker section of the beach. In all of his years, he'd never made love on a beach. It might be time to rectify that.

A man approached, forcing Cornelius and Tricia to act civilized.

"Hey, Danny," Tricia said, smoothing her hair back.

The young man smiled shyly. "Hey, Tricia. Is this Dennis?"

Cornelius extended his hand. "Dennis McCready, at your service. Are you manning the grill over there?"

"I am," Danny replied. "Do you have something for me in that bag?"

He gestured to the insulated bag slung over Cornelius' shoulder, then reached out to take it off his hands.

"Hushpuppies, okra, wine, and mead," Cornelius explained. "I hope they'll do."

"That's fantastic," Danny said. He seemed genuinely grateful for the contribution.

Tricia leaned toward Danny, being a good hostess. "Danny lives on the other side of the island, near the Pitt Street Bridge. He and his wife have a gorgeous waterfront property. I'll point it out to you sometime, Dennis."

"I'd like that," Cornelius said, his attention back on Tricia.

He found it hard to tear his gaze away from her. The way she moved made it seem like she'd be good in bed.

Sensing the sexual tension, Danny said thanks again and made his exit.

Other people introduced themselves, coming and going as Tricia led Cornelius through the crowd. It was a friendly group, and for the first time in a long time, Cornelius felt like this place could be a home. He'd always assumed that he'd go back to Appleman's Gap once The Cradler was brought to justice. But a different plan began to niggle at him. What if he stayed here, in the Charleston area? The weather was nice, the people were friendly, the food was good, and the women were beautiful. The place was really growing on him.

Maureen didn't seem interested in a reconciliation, anyway. From what Cornelius had heard, his wife of nearly forty years had moved on with Mack Roberts. When he'd contacted her to let her know he was alive and well, working undercover, she had yelled at him and hung up the phone. It was sad, but what could he do? A man could only spend so much time grieving a relationship when the woman was no longer in love with him.

His attention was brought back to the present as Tricia held a bottle of beer in front of her.

"Try this," she said. "Charleston has some top-notch craft breweries. This one is from a place on Calhoun Street, downtown. Right near the house I lived in when I was in college."

She popped the top and took a swig, then handed the bottle to Cornelius.

"College of Charleston?" he asked as he took a long drink.

He knew he needed to be careful and not become inebriated, but the beer tasted good and the endorphins were flowing.

"That's right," she said. "I was a business major back before it was cool."

He laughed, taking another drink. "I'd bet that you, Tricia Bowers, were always cool."

"Tell that to my roommates who threw a party every weekend and invited Citadel guys. I usually stayed in my room to study while the music blared on the other side of my door."

"What did you do with your fancy business degree?" he asked.

She sighed, twirling a section of hair like a younger

woman might. "I went to get an MBA at the University of South Carolina."

Cornelius drank again, polishing off the rest of the bottle. "That's in Columbia, right?"

It was time for him to roll out the Dennis McCready backstory he'd been rehearsing. It would soon become obvious that he wasn't a Charleston native.

Tricia chuckled, then led Cornelius to a chair and plopped herself onto his lap. Somehow, another bottle of beer appeared in her hand and she urged him to drink. He did.

"Yes, silly, it's in Columbia. Where are you from, anyway?"

"Pennsylvania," he lied. "Amish country in the eastern part of the state. A little town called Lancaster. It's about an hour from Philadelphia, or *Filthydelphia* as a buddy of mine used to call it."

"Was your family Amish?"

"Not hardly," he replied, taking another drink of beer. "More alcoholic than anything. My dad had a real drinking problem when I was growing up. He got mean."

That part was true. No embellishment required.

"I'm sorry," she said, leaning her head on his shoulder. "I don't want to make you sad. I shouldn't have asked so many personal questions."

"That's okay," Cornelius said as he let one hand rest low on her hip. "I'm enjoying spending time with you."

"Me, too," she replied, lifting her head just enough to whisper against his cheek.

"LAUREL, HONEY, WAKE UP. PLEASE."

Maureen Dane's voice was full of concern as it blared from the speakers in Brad's truck.

"Mom? What's going on?" Laurel asked as she came to. She was groggy, her mind toggling in and out of consciousness.

She had a fuzzy memory of seeing Brad pounding on someone as they cowered on the ground, then of Mikey carrying her in his arms like she was a baby. None of that made sense. Was she imagining things?

"Thank God," Maureen said. "I'm so glad to hear your voice. Ever since Brad called me, I've been as nervous as a long-tailed cat in a room full of rocking chairs."

"I'm okay," Laurel said, although she wasn't completely sure that was true.

"She's coming to," Mikey said.

Laurel couldn't tell which direction her brother's voice was coming from, but hearing it made her feel safer. Suddenly, she remembered that she was pregnant. It was a strange thing to forget, even for a second. Yet, she had. That spoke to how hard she'd been hit on the head.

"Is the baby okay?" she asked frantically, touching her belly.

"He or she is fine, Sis," Mikey said. "When you fell, you landed on that big butt of yours. The little one didn't get the impact."

"You'd better take good care of my grandchild," Maureen said, choking up. "Every last one of y'all is precious to me."

Laurel finally became aware of Mikey's position. He was standing outside the passenger door of Brad's truck as she reclined inside.

"Wait!" Laurel said, panicked. "Where's Brad? Is he okay?"

"He's good," Mikey said. "But you should see the other guy. Brad has him in zip ties while waiting for local police. An ample amount of blood was shed."

Releasing a big breath, Laurel relaxed. "Okay," she said, finally able to breathe normally. "Lilly?"

Right on cue, the pup placed her front paws on the center console and nuzzled Laurel's arm.

"I think she's worried about you," Mikey explained. "Otherwise, she's fine."

"Good."

With lucid consciousness returning, Laurel thought about the intricacies of her situation. Who were the man and woman who had coordinated the attack on her? Had it been random?

"Laurel?" Maureen asked over the speakers, her voice still booming because the volume was turned up so loud.

"Yeah?"

"Does your daddy know what's going on?"

Mother and daughter had not acknowledged to each other the fact that Cornelius was alive, much less discussed details of Laurel's visit to see him in South Carolina.

"I don't think so," Laurel replied. "Unless Brad or Mikey called him. We're less than fifteen minutes from the house where he's staying. He'll probably be wondering what's taking us so long."

"Let me let you go," Maureen said. "I'll call back to check on you later."

"Okay."

"Mikey, be a good boy and take care of your big sister," Maureen said. "Keep an eye on her like a hawk on a rabbit."

She disconnected the call as both Laurel and Mikey smiled.

Maureen was quite the distinctive character. She loved her family fiercely. Talking to her for a few minutes had made them all feel better.

Mikey extended his hand to help Laurel out of the truck, if she wanted to stand. "Want some fresh air?" he asked.

"Is it safe?" she asked, glancing around the parking lot.

She could see where a small crowd had gathered near the bathroom pavilion. She assumed that's where Brad was holding the attackers. It was almost dark, and the lack of visibility made her nervous. Laurel had to admit, though, seeing lights as they reflected off the water was beautiful. The bridge looked pretty all lit up against the night sky, too.

"It's safe with me by your side," Mikey said, flexing a bicep for show. "Come on. We can sit on one of those benches near the water and chat. I want to hear what happened in there."

Reluctantly, Laurel agreed. She leashed Lilly and the two of them stepped carefully out of the truck, under Mikey's watchful eye. They locked the truck and made their way to a bench. As she sat gingerly on the bench, Laurel realized that both her head and her backside hurt. She was going to have bruises.

"Ouch," she said.

"Is it your head?" Mikey asked. "We should probably get that checked out."

"It hurts, but I think my butt might actually hurt more," she said with a laugh. "Apparently, it wasn't big enough to properly cushion my fall."

"Better do some more squats," Mikey said.

"I'll get right on it," Laurel replied, glancing toward the bathrooms. She wouldn't completely relax until the attackers had been taken away and Brad was back.

Lilly stayed close, positioning herself by Laurel's side.

"So, what happened?" Mikey asked.

Laurel replayed the scene from her memory, explaining how she'd had a bad feeling from the time she'd entered the bathroom. She told her brother how the woman seemed to signal the man and how, together, they managed to trap her. She told him about the blow to the head and how everything went black.

"How did you and Brad know to come to my aid?" she asked. "I was almost ready to yell for you guys, but never got the chance."

"Thank your man candy," Mikey said. "It was all him. Brad thought he heard you raise your voice, so he and I went to stand outside of the women's bathroom. He suspected you might be in trouble. His hunch turned out to be right, which we confirmed when we saw a guy carrying you over his shoulder. You were limp, your limbs dangling. Suffice to say, Brad and I didn't appreciate that. We jumped into action."

"The guy was carrying me?" Laurel asked.

"He was."

"I have zero memory of that. How disturbing," she said.

Mikey nodded. "I got hold of you and took you and Lilly back to the truck while Brad handled the scumbag. I could tell he wouldn't need my help. It looked like Brad was ripping the guy apart with his bare hands."

"Wow."

Laurel was concerned, but she was also proud. Brad and Mikey had come through for her in a huge way. She'd always known they would. It was quite amazing for it to have actually happened, though. Who knows where she'd be right now if not for their intervention?

"I would have done it if Brad hadn't," Mikey added. "I'd do the same for Jess or our girls. Or Mom or Maggie or Hazel. Even for Ryan, should our little brother find himself in need. You don't mess with family."

"I agree," Laurel said. "I just don't understand why this kind of thing keeps happening to me. Am I cursed or something?"

"I doubt that," Mikey replied, shrugging a shoulder. "I can't help but wonder if this is connected to everything else, though."

"The Cradler?" Laurel asked, her eyes wide.

"It's a possibility, isn't it?"

That thought hadn't occurred to Laurel yet, but her brother was right. Someone could have followed them here, waiting on an opportunity to grab her. If that was the case, it could mean that they inadvertently gave away clues about Cornelius' location, too.

"God, I hope not," Laurel said. "I'd rather it was random. I'd hate to think The Cradler would go to these lengths."

"Why wouldn't he? He's proven how depraved he is by kidnapping and killing multiple people. Anyone who targets pregnant women, mothers, and babies is scum of the Earth to begin with," Mikey said. "I think you've gone soft, Sis. You're giving him too much credit."

"You're probably right."

Just then, the cavalry arrived. No less than six police cruisers with flashing lights pulled into the parking lot and surrounded the bathroom pavilion. A male and female officer from the lead car jumped out with guns drawn and handcuffs at the ready. The remainder of the officers did various tasks to set up a perimeter.

"I hope they know Brad is the good guy," Laurel said.

"They do," her brother replied. "These are his people. Police share a brother and sisterhood, no matter where they are in the country. Don't worry. They'll know he's one of their own."

Laurel nodded.

"They're going to want you to provide a statement," Mikey said. "You know the drill."

Laurel was well aware, but hadn't thought about that yet as it pertained to this situation. Her thoughts were still sluggish.

"I really don't want to spend my evening at a police station," she said. "I'm exhausted from the trip, and now sore. Maybe Jimmy can get me out of it. Has anyone called him? He should have touched down in Nashville by now."

Mikey shook his head. "Good idea. Go ahead."

Remembering that she'd seen her handbag in the truck, the plan to call her boss stalled. "Dammit," she complained. "I don't have my phone with me."

"That's okay," Mikey said, gesturing to a pair of officers walking their direction. "Looks like they're coming to take a statement from you, anyway. Let's see what they say. I'll run back to the truck and grab your phone in a bit, if I need to."

Lilly barked protectively as the officers approached, placing herself between Laurel and the men in uniform.

"It's okay, Lilly," Laurel said. "Good girl."

The dog quieted reluctantly, keeping a watchful eye on her favorite human.

Laurel steeled herself, as ready as she could be for whatever might come her way.

PART TWO

Changes of Plans

Ten

"DIDN'T you say you were bringing guests?" Tricia asked.

It had been what felt like a long while as she and Cornelius sat curled against each other, enjoying the sounds of the waves crashing nearby. It was getting colder as the sun retreated for the night. Thanks to their body heat, they were warm and cozy.

Cornelius had nearly forgotten about his family arriving soon, what with the beer—he'd had at least four within the hour—and the enticing company. He knew they'd get there when they could. He wouldn't want to pressure them in any way.

"They must be running late," he said. "Are we eating soon?"

"We could ask Danny to be sure," Tricia said, "but I'd guess yes. It smells like all kinds of good stuff is almost ready. Should you call your friends?"

"That isn't a bad idea," Cornelius said. He stood, gently sliding Tricia off his lap and onto her own feet. "I'll be right back."

He walked a few yards toward the ocean. He didn't want anyone to overhear his conversation. Even if he kept it brief and impersonal, he preferred privacy. He couldn't be too careful.

Before he could find Laurel's number and dial, his phone buzzed with an incoming call. He'd recognize the number anywhere. It was Maureen, calling from the landline at their home.

"What the hell?" he mused, the intoxication from the beer making it hard to judge exactly how loud he was talking.

A trio of young women sitting around a firepit looked his way. He waved them off, moving closer to the water. When he felt certain he wouldn't be overheard, he pushed the button to answer the call, then placed the phone against his ear.

"Hello?" he asked.

"Cornelius Dane," Maureen began, her tone scolding. "Have you been drinking? I swear, you've got more nerve than sense."

"Good evening to you, too," he said. He could hear his words slurring ever so slightly. Maureen knew him well enough that she'd notice.

"Do you know where your daughter is?" she asked.

"Which daughter? I had three, last time I checked."

Maureen's voice became even more cross. "Make that four, if you count Sarah. You must be dumb as a bag of hammers. I'm talking about Laurel. The daughter who is on her way to visit you at your swanky beach house in South Carolina."

"Maureen, you ought not say those things out loud," he replied, growing frustrated. "Is he there with you, listening?"

She hesitated, deciding how to respond. "No, he's not.

Laurel is in trouble. She was attacked at some park in Mount Pleasant. Said she was less than fifteen minutes from the house you're staying in."

"What? Is she all right?" he asked, becoming concerned as he thought back to Jimmy's call from that morning and the mysterious informant.

Would someone target Laurel if they were trying to get at him? Maybe.

"She's shaken up and has a banged head, but she's okay," Maureen explained. "Brad and Mikey took care of the man who attacked her. I expect that the police are there now, doing their thing."

"What should I do?" he asked.

It was a preposterous question. Cornelius had been a longtime police chief in Appleman's Gap. With his background in law enforcement, Maureen should have been asking him what to do, not the other way around. Yet in his distressed and somewhat intoxicated state, he wasn't sure what to think. He wanted his wife to take the lead and give him his marching orders.

"You're acting crazier than a sprayed roach," Maureen mused.

Cornelius smiled. He'd missed his wife and her funny sayings. For a moment, his emotions were all over the place. He was worried about Laurel, nostalgic for the woman who'd been his partner for four decades, and intensely drawn to the two new women he had met in Charleston.

"Are they on their way to my house?" he asked.

"Well, gee, I don't know if they can get there as planned, Cornelius," she said. "How about you go to them? Unless you're too afraid to be seen with them out in public. I don't know what level of cover you're working under."

"Good point," he said.

"And you've been drinking. You shouldn't drive."

She was right about that, too. He couldn't exactly ask Tricia to drive him to meet up with Laurel either. Or could he? No, that was a bad idea. He nixed it promptly.

"I could call a cab, or a rideshare," he tried.

"Figure it out," Maureen said. "Call me back and let me know our girl is okay ... when you see her with your own eyes. If I don't hear from you by tomorrow morning, I'm getting in the car myself."

He raised his brows. That didn't sound so awful. He'd love to see Maureen again. Maybe they'd have a chance to talk things through.

"Okay," he said, but she'd already disconnected the call.

It was just in time, because Tricia had grown curious and was looking his way. Cornelius had to think fast. What would he tell her? He wished he hadn't had so much beer.

He walked quickly to where the crowd was gathered under the lights, then turned to face her.

"Everything all right?" she asked, her brow furrowed.

"Just got a call about a friend who's in a bit of a pickle," Cornelius said, trying to keep his voice steady despite the alcohol. "I need to go check on them."

"Oh my goodness, I'm so sorry," Tricia said, reaching out to touch his arm. "Do you need help? I can drive you. My car is here."

Cornelius shook his head. "No, no, it's fine. I'll call a rideshare."

Before he could pull out his phone again, Cornelius noticed a man walking towards them from the shadows. He could tell the man was tall and light-skinned. That's about all he could discern. The man's face was partially obscured by the brim of a baseball cap, but something about his posture and the way he moved set off alarm bells in Cornelius' mind. His vibe didn't fit with a neighborhood fish fry. Something was wrong.

"Tricia, step back," Cornelius said quietly, pushing her behind him.

"What is it?" she asked, her voice tinged with fear.

The man kept advancing, reaching into his jacket. Cornelius' instincts kicked in. He quickly assessed his surroundings and saw a nearby table laden with food. In one swift motion, he flipped the table over, sending plates and cutlery flying. The table landed between him and the approaching man just as a silenced pistol appeared in the man's hand.

His instinct had been right.

The first muffled shot hit the table, splintering the wood. People around them screamed and scattered, creating chaos. Poor Danny looked horrified as the food he had meticulously prepared was slung around the beach. Cornelius grabbed Tricia's hand and pulled her down behind the overturned table, using it as cover.

"Stay down!" he shouted, his voice cutting through the panic.

From his position, Cornelius could see the man's feet moving closer. He had to act fast. Grabbing a heavy metal serving tray from the ground, Cornelius waited until the shooter was close enough, then he hurled the tray with all his might. It struck the man in the knees, causing him to stumble.

Taking advantage of the momentary distraction, Cornelius sprang up and tackled the shooter, wrestling the gun from his hand. They struggled on the sand, the assassin fighting fiercely. Somehow, it was still hard for Cornelius to note any identifying features. This guy could blend into a crowd, which is exactly what he had done. Finally, Cornelius managed to land a solid punch to the man's jaw, disorienting him.

Just as Cornelius was about to subdue the shooter completely, he heard a familiar voice.

"Freeze! F.B.I.!" Laurel shouted, a gun drawn and aimed at the man on the ground.

Brad and Mikey were right behind her, securing the perimeter and ensuring the crowd was safe. Laurel moved swiftly, cuffing the would-be assassin while Brad and Mikey checked for any other threats.

Cornelius stood up, breathing heavily, and wiped the sand from his hands. He looked at his daughter, who was clearly shaken but determined. He liked seeing her in Agent Dane mode. She was a badass.

"Are you okay?" Laurel asked, her eyes filled with concern. She was careful not to refer to him as her father, but Cornelius could tell it was on the tip of her tongue.

"Yeah, I'm fine," Cornelius replied, his voice steady. "No worse for wear. Thanks for the backup. Perfect timing."

Tricia, who had been watching in stunned silence, finally found her voice. "What just happened? Dennis, who was that man?"

Cornelius sighed, thinking quickly. "Just an old enemy

from my past. It's complicated. But now isn't the time for explanations."

Laurel stepped forward, nodding to Tricia. "We need to get Dennis to a safe place. This isn't over yet. As long as you're with him, you're in danger, too."

Cornelius nodded, grateful for his daughter's quick thinking. "Tricia, I need you to trust me. I can't explain everything right now, but I'll be in touch when I can. The evening was lovely. Thanks for inviting me."

Tricia, still shocked, nodded slowly. "Just be careful, okay?"

Cornelius gave her a reassuring smile. "I will."

As they moved to leave, Cornelius glanced back at the crowd, hoping that the evening's chaos hadn't put too many people in danger. With Laurel, Brad, and Mikey by his side, he knew they had a lot of work ahead of them. The Cradler's syndicate was closing in, and they needed to stay one step ahead.

In what can only be described as laughable timing, Cornelius' phone buzzed with an incoming text message. It was from Jimmy.

You're burned. Get out immediately.

"Yeah, you think?" Cornelius mused as he read it.

He climbed into Brad's big blue truck with his kids, then they drove away. This wasn't the reunion any of them had in mind.

Eleven

AS BRAD SPED AWAY from the beach, the adrenaline from the attacks began to wear off, and Laurel's anger started to bubble to the surface. Cornelius was talking to Lilly in the backseat, and Laurel wanted to smack him. How could he act like this was a happy family gathering after what had just happened—to him at the fish fry and to her in the bathroom at the park?

Things had escalated to a seriously dangerous level.

"What the hell were you thinking, Dad?" Laurel asked. "Drinking at a public event when you know you're being hunted? You could have gotten yourself killed."

"Laurel, I—"

"No, don't 'Laurel' me. This isn't just about you anymore. What if that woman had gotten hurt? Tricia, right? Or any of those innocent people at the fish fry? You're not some lone wolf hero. You have a family that needs you. *We* need you."

Cornelius sighed, realizing how deeply he'd messed up. "I know. I'm sorry. I just needed a break. I've been working alone for months, and I was going stir crazy. I decided it was a reasonable strategy to get to know some locals. That way, if my face made national news, they could say that I was just a regular guy."

"Forgive me for interjecting, Chief," Brad said, "but what good would that do?"

"I don't know," Cornelius said. "I read it in a Stephen King novel."

"You can't be serious," Laurel huffed.

"Oh, I read that one," Mikey said. "About the sniper who pretended to be writing a book while he waited to make his kill, right?"

Cornelius nodded. "That's the one. *Billy Summers.*"

"Right. Granted, Dad," Mikey said, "there were some key differences."

"Yeah, I know," Cornelius said. "I guess I really needed some social interaction."

"Or did you want to get laid?" Laurel asked.

Mikey and Brad smiled. They couldn't help themselves. They both appreciated Laurel's feisty personality, and they were glad to see her feeling strong and assertive. Both had worried that she'd retreat inside herself after this evening's attack at the park. Anger was a healthier response.

"You know," she continued, despite her Dad's silence, "Mom thinks you're a womanizer. I've always defended you, but at this point I'm inclined to agree. It seems your every decision lately revolves around some woman you're pursuing."

"Easy, Sis," Mikey said. "We're all a little shaken up right now. How about we focus on where we're staying tonight."

Laurel waved a hand in the air. "Stay wherever you want. I have things to say. I've been holding them in for far too long."

"Go ahead," Cornelius said to his daughter, nodding. He looked like a prison of war, bracing for impact as the bad guys set out their instruments of torture. "Get everything off your chest. I have it coming."

Laurel huffed. "Are you even sober enough to remember what I'll say?"

"I think so. It was just a few beers."

"Sure, it was," she said.

She turned in the passenger seat so that she could look him in the eye. Shadows moved across their faces as they passed under tall street lights on their way north on Highway 17. Laurel honestly didn't care where they were heading. She was so mad at her dad, she could spit. Or cry. Or something. She was furious.

"You've always been so stubborn, Dad. And reckless. But this time, it's different. We're dealing with people who don't just want you dead—they want all of us gone. This isn't just about you anymore. You need to start thinking about us, about our safety. About your grandchildren."

She didn't specifically name Jasper, but they all knew who she was referring to. Only now, her own baby would be one of Cornelius' grandchildren at risk.

"I know, Laurel. I really do. And I'm sorry. I've been so focused on trying to end this once and for all that I didn't realize how much I was putting all of you at risk. I'll do better. I promise. Please, don't be mad at me."

"It isn't that simple," Brad said.

Brad wanted to let Laurel and her dad each have their say with each other, but the truth was that keeping Cornelius' secrets had put a strain on his relationship with Laurel, too. Brad was involved in this thing, whether he liked it or not.

They rode in silence for a while, the city lights fading as they traveled the open stretch of four-lane road between Charleston and Myrtle Beach. Laurel thought her dad might have been napping in the backseat, he was so quiet. Finally, he broke the silence.

"Lilly is a really nice dog," he said, scratching behind one of her ears.

Lilly smiled in response, letting herself be putty in Cornelius' hands.

"She likes you," Mikey said, smiling.

Mikey, no doubt, had feelings about everything that had happened with their dad. He wasn't ready to air them.

"I saw a black lab out on the beach this morning," Cornelius said, "and it made me want to get one someday. Once things settle down, of course. I'll name him Sully, for my time on Sullivan's Island."

Laurel couldn't help but soften at that. They were a family of animal lovers, and it had been a long time since her dad had a dog.

"Like Raven?" she asked.

Raven had been a beautiful black lab that the Dane family had owned when Laurel and her siblings were little. She'd been a great dog, watchful and loyal.

"As a matter of fact, yes," Cornelius said. His body language was more relaxed now as he gently stroked Lilly's head. "Raven was a great girl. I'd be lucky to have another dog like her. Can't you see my Sully traipsing through the orchards at home, tail wagging happily?"

"You think you're going back home to the orchards?" Laurel asked, the frustration returning to her voice.

"Hopefully, someday."

Laurel looked at Brad, then rolled her eyes.

"I think you have a lot of ground to cover between here and there," she said, "and I don't just mean miles on the interstate."

"Mom is pretty pissed at you," Mikey said. "She's called you more than a few colorful names since we found out that you weren't actually a dead man. Can you blame her? She was grieving you. Taking it pretty hard, too."

"I get it," Cornelius said.

There was another break in the conversation as they stared at the dark road ahead, each lost in their own thoughts.

"So, where are we going for the night?" Cornelius asked.

"Oak Island, North Carolina," Brad said. "It's not far past the state line. Jimmy has a safe house secured. We'll stay there for a night or two, then return home, whenever he's ready for us. You'll be kept out of sight at all times, Cornelius. It's time to act like a dead man."

"Jimmy must really like the beach," Cornelius said. "Can't complain about that."

Mikey nodded his approval.

"Did he say if he'll send an Agent to get my things from Sullivan's Island? My computer is secured as well as possible, but if someone who knows what they're doing gets their hands on it, it could mean trouble for the investigation."

"I'm sure he'll send someone," Laurel said. "The F.B.I. wants that data as much as you do. Maybe more."

"Understood."

"Any other questions?" Brad asked, eying Cornelius in the rearview mirror.

"Actually, yes. Shouldn't we get Laurel checked out? Maureen told me she was hit in the head."

Laurel whipped around to face her dad. "Mom called you?"

"Of course," he replied. "You're our baby girl, no matter how big you get. Our differences are nothing when it comes to your wellbeing."

That sentiment touched Laurel, and she began to tear up. Seeing her emotion, Brad reached out and took her hand.

"Thank you," she said simply to her dad as she squeezed Brad's hand.

"I think she's okay, Chief," Brad said to Cornelius. "Medics checked her out. They gave us a list of symptoms to look out for. As long as she doesn't exhibit any of that mess, she's good. We'll keep a close watch."

Cornelius nodded, satisfied.

Just then, an incoming call from Jimmy interrupted their conversation. Laurel handed her phone to Brad, who connected it through the speaker system in his truck.

"Hey Jimmy," she said. "We're all here. Dad, too. Heading north to Oak Island. We have a few hours to go."

"Good," he replied. "I'll be in touch tomorrow morning with a proper update. Get to the safe house and lay low. The kitchen is already stocked. For now, though, I wanted to let you know that forensics identified the body we found in Cedar Hollow."

Laurel held her breath, afraid that Jimmy would say it was Kanesha's sister. She really hoped it wasn't Tiana.

"And?" Brad asked.

"Tiana Sneed Douglas," he said. "I'm sorry. Laurel, I know you're friends with her sister."

It felt like Laurel had been punched in the gut. She cradled her own baby bump protectively. "Aww, no," she said. "I hate to hear that."

"They're fairly confident that the baby was alive when he or she was removed from Tiana's womb. Our focus now is to find that missing baby. We've issued an Amber Alert and are doing everything we can. Tiana would want that. Not to mention, the baby's father, Paul, is distraught."

"I don't blame him," Brad said.

The phone crackled on Jimmy's end, as if he was covering the receiver to mask some background noise. When the sound became clear again, Jimmy had a final warning.

"Laurel, I'll need you on your A-game when you get back here. Rest up, and get ready."

Twelve

THE SAFE HOUSE WAS NICE. Laurel wasn't sure if Jimmy was the one choosing and furnishing the houses, but she was impressed with how comfortable the accommodations were. White shiplap lined the walls as ceiling fans with blades made to look like palm leaves moved lazily in each room.

They'd been in Oak Island for a few days. This morning, Cornelius was sitting at the breakfast table, slicing a banana as the pieces dropped into his bowl of oatmeal. He'd borrowed some athletic shorts and a t-shirt from Mikey while the only outfit he owned at the moment was laundered for a second time.

Good thing Cornelius and his oldest son were about the same size. Brad was several inches taller and considerably broader. His clothes might have made Cornelius appear like a kid wearing a grown-up's outfit.

It was dreary outside, and the drizzle had dampened Laurel's mood. She was apprehensive about returning home to Appleman's Gap and going back to work. At the same time, though, she was eager to get moving on the most recent kidnapping case. What had happened to Kanesha's sister was horrific. Laurel desperately wanted to find Tiana's baby and return him or her to the family safely.

"Was your place on Sullivan's Island this nice?" she asked her dad.

"Nicer," he said. "Jimmy knows how to do it right. Wish you were able to see my house down there."

"Me, too," she replied. "We were all looking forward to spending time in Charleston."

He chuckled. "I'll do you one better. I had a list of tourist hot spots I wanted us to hit."

"Oh, really? Was the downtown City Market on your list? Because I had plans to buy some sweetgrass baskets to bring home. Maybe I'm nesting."

Cornelius smiled and leaned back in his chair, beaming with pride. "My baby girl is so grown up, expecting a baby of her own."

Laurel blushed. "I've been grown up for quite a while now, Dad."

He shrugged. "Not this grown up."

She sliced an apple, then slathered the pieces with a spoonful of peanut butter.

"To answer your question," Cornelius continued, "yes, I'd hoped we could stop at the City Market. It's the best place to get those sweetgrass baskets, t-shirts, and fudge, all in the same spot. A carriage ride might have been fun, after."

"Not if it rained like this," she said, gesturing to the sliding glass doors that framed the beach scene out back. "At least, it's much warmer than January typically is back home."

"Yet Appleman's Gap is way warmer than D.C. is this

time of year," Brad added as he entered the room. "It's all relative."

He walked up behind Laurel, wrapped an arm around her, slowly moved her hair out of the way, and kissed the back of her neck.

"True," she agreed as she turned and returned his kiss.

"Say, have you two lovebirds set a date for the wedding yet?" Cornelius asked. "I hope to be out of hiding by then—and still alive—so that I can attend. I want to walk you down the aisle, Laurel."

Laurel's brow lowered, a look of concern on her face. "Why wouldn't you be alive, Dad?"

Cornelius shrugged. "A hunch, maybe. I'm not sure. The Cradler would like to see me dead. I suspect things will get much worse before they get better."

There was an uncomfortable silence. No one knew quite what to say about that. What do you say when a person has a hunch they're going to die? Nothing.

"We haven't set a wedding date," Brad said, steering the conversation. He didn't want to see Laurel upset again. "There's been a lot going on, including a certain young woman staying in my carriage house."

Cornelius' eyes went wide, but he quickly got them under control. He laced his fingers together, then stared down at the floor. "Oh," he said.

It seemed like Cornelius hadn't realized the effect that particular guest might have on his daughter. He should've known.

"Moving on," Laurel said. "I don't want to get into all of that."

"Understood," Brad replied as he poured some cereal into

a bowl. The toasted pieces clanked softly against the porcelain. "Do we have our marching orders from Jimmy yet? We're heading home today, right?"

There had been no more disruptions since the events of Saturday evening. It was Tuesday now, and Laurel, Brad, and Cornelius all wanted to do something useful instead of sit around in a safe house. Even Mikey, who didn't work in law enforcement, was eager to use his hacking skills to contribute. They were looking to Jimmy to direct their next moves.

"Waiting on his call," Laurel said.

Mikey joined them, his hair still damp from the shower. "What did I miss?" he asked as he took a seat at the breakfast table.

"Nothing much, son," Cornelius said.

Mikey softened hearing his dad use the term of endearment. He'd missed the old man.

Brad brought his cereal to the table and sat down next to Mikey. "I'm thinking we should compare notes. Like seriously, hash it all out and make a plan. I don't mean to go around Jimmy, but Jimmy isn't family. I say we circle the wagons and make sure things are solid amongst this group, right here."

"He's a friend who's like family," Laurel added. "But I get what you mean. That isn't a bad idea. Maybe we're not being aggressive enough in tackling the problem."

"The problem of The Cradler?" Mikey asked.

"That's the one," Brad said. "It's the biggest problem my department faces, for sure. Everything else comes to a halt when a community faces a threat of that magnitude."

Cornelius laughed. "Yeah, it was the biggest problem my

department faced for damn near three decades. The Cradler and his father, Lucian."

"It's one of the biggest problems the F.B.I. faces," Laurel said. "We don't get that many kidnappings for ransom here in the States anymore. We certainly don't have babies being cut from their mothers' wombs. Horrible."

She sat down at the table, too, completing the group.

"We're all here with time to kill," Brad said. "How about we treat this like our own task force and help each other out?"

Mikey nodded to Brad. "I'm game, but aren't you too much of a Boy Scout to go around the rules like that? What you're proposing isn't exactly by the book."

Brad shifted his weight. It seemed like he wanted to say more than he thought he should. "Maybe I'm concerned about my growing family," he said softly. "Their safety and wellbeing is enough motivation to bend the rules, if that's what it takes to get things done."

"Atta boy," Cornelius said, leaning forward to give Brad a high five.

Laurel squeezed Brad's hand. "I'm the one who stands to be in the most trouble here. The Bureau doesn't take kindly to information being shared, and that includes with local police chiefs. They like to keep a tight lid on everything, if at all possible."

"Sis, are you willing to risk it?" Mikey asked. "We've talked about this before. You could be risking your career. That's a big deal."

Laurel shrugged. "Like I told you, I'm not completely sure I want to be an F.B.I. agent forever. If things go sideways and I burn that bridge, well, it might be for the best in the long run. I've been seriously considering a career as a private investigator. I like the idea of doing things my own way."

"We could form our own agency," Cornelius said. "If you'd want to go into business with your old dad, that is."

"Really?" Laurel asked. "You'd be interested in doing that with me?"

"Absolutely," Cornelius replied. "One hundred percent."

"I'd have to talk to Jess first," Mikey added, "but assuming she was okay with it, I'd be in."

Laurel's face lit up. "Wait. Seriously? You'd both want to work with me?"

They nodded.

"Sounds like the Dane Detective Agency is off and running," Brad said.

Laurel gave him a knowing look. "And you?"

It took Brad a minute to realize what she was asking. "Oh," he said, when it finally dawned on him. "I'm just settling into my job as Chief. I'm not sure I'd be ready to leave it anytime soon. Maybe?"

"Let him be Chief," Cornelius said. "Having Brad in the role would be beneficial to us. What if his replacement wasn't as friendly?"

Laurel moved on, giving her dad and brother her full attention. "We'd be based in Appleman's Gap?"

Mikey shrugged this time. "Talking Jess into moving away from Knoxville might be more difficult. Can I work remotely? Most of what I'd handle for us would be done alone in front of my computer anyway. I could come to Appleman's Gap a couple of times per week if we needed to consult in person. It's doable. In fact, my presence in East Tennessee might expand our agency's reach. We could set up an office there and I could handle intake for new clients in the region."

"I like it," Cornelius said. "If you haven't noticed," he continued, clearing his throat dramatically then laughing, "the job I held for many years has been filled. Some young hothead, I hear."

"Yeah, yeah," Brad said, laughing, too.

"I guess I'd have to officially move home from Washington, D.C.," Laurel mused.

"Um, and leave the Bureau," Brad said. "Don't forget that minor detail."

"Yeah."

Finishing his oatmeal, Cornelius returned the spoon to the bowl with a jangle. "I assume you want to work this case for the Bureau first. Right?"

"I've already committed to helping Jimmy," Laurel said. "So, yes. Once The Cradler is put behind bars, then it might just be time for a change of pace. Come to think of it, one of my closest friends back in D.C. was a private investigator before she joined the F.B.I."

"Della Brady?" Brad asked.

"Yes," Laurel said. "I'm doing it backwards, I suppose. It probably makes more sense for a private investigator to transition to the Bureau, rather than vice versa. The skills and experience gained in private investigation can be appealing to the F.B.I., especially if the individual has demonstrated exceptional investigative abilities and a strong understanding of legal processes. Della definitely did both during the early part of her career. She'd be a great person to ask for advice."

"I'm not sure there's a right or a wrong way," Brad

replied. "There are advantages to both routes. Don't be too hard on yourself, babe. You're doing great."

"I agree," Cornelius said. "Talk to your friend Della. Mull it over."

Laurel leaned forward and looked hard at her dad and brother. "You two are completely serious about going into business with me?"

"Totally," Mikey said.

"I can't imagine a better plan," Cornelius confirmed. "The Dane Family Detective Agency has a nice ring to it."

Thirteen

JIMMY CALLED that afternoon with detailed instructions for the four of them.

Laurel and Brad would return to work in Appleman's Gap the following day. They'd drive home in Brad's truck, since Jimmy was relatively confident that no one was following them anymore. The men who had attacked Laurel and Cornelius in Charleston were in custody. Plus, Laurel and Brad were trained to defend themselves. Jimmy mentioned that securing additional firepower couldn't hurt, and he gave them an address in nearby Wilmington where they could take care of the matter. Surveillance had already been set up at Brad's house in Appleman's Gap. There had been no sign of trouble.

Mikey would return to his normal life in Knoxville, albeit a few days earlier than originally planned. Jimmy hadn't assigned him any Bureau-sponsored surveillance or protection, but he stood ready to do so, should the situation escalate.

Things were a bit more complicated for Cornelius, on

the other hand. He would take a private plane from Wilmington, North Carolina and would be hidden for a few days while the Bureau finished preparations on the safe house near Appleman's Gap and ensured a discreet arrival. Jimmy explained that using a private plane was his preferred method for high-risk witnesses as it provided more control over the environment and reduced exposure to potential threats.

"So, I'm a high risk-witness?" Cornelius had asked.

They had all looked at him, as if to say, "duh."

That evening, they were lounging around the safe house, growing restless after having been cooped up for several days. They had just settled around the big, wooden dining table to have the first-ever meeting of their new family task force when Laurel's phone buzzed. She glanced at the screen and saw Della Brady's name flashing.

"Speak of the devil," she said with a smile, answering the call.

"Della! What's up, stranger?"

"Hey, Laurel. I heard about your dad's situation and wanted to check in. Are you all holding up okay?"

"We're managing," Laurel replied. "Actually, I was just talking about you earlier today. Were your ears burning?"

Della laughed, that deep, hearty laugh that everyone who knew her loved. Laurel could almost see her friend's long, thick, dark hair bouncing eagerly around her shoulders as she leaned her head back to laugh. Della was an intense woman. In many ways, her strong personality was a good match for Laurel's. In others, their differences complimented each other.

"Maybe that was it," Della replied. "A disturbance in the

force, or something. I'm no Star Wars expert, but isn't that how it works?"

Laurel agreed. "Something like that."

Laurel stood and stepped out onto the screened porch on the back of the house, while Brad explained to the others that she always liked to talk in private when Della was on the line. "Not sure if it's a F.B.I. thing, or just a weird girly thing," he said.

"Probably weird girly," Mikey agreed with a laugh, popping a handful of pistachios into his mouth.

Out on the porch, Laurel relaxed, for the first time in a while. She hadn't talked to Della in months—just a series of text messages. It felt good to hear her friend's voice. She told Della about the carjacking and kidnapping of Baby Jasper, about everything that had been happening with Brad and Jamie, and about the attack at the park in Charleston.

"Goodness, Laurel," Della said. "You've really been through it. Your texts made your situation sound manageable, but this doesn't sound so manageable when I hear the details."

Tears sprung to Laurel's eyes. She'd been putting on a brave face, especially for the past few days. Not that the brave face was phony. It was very real. But she needed to let off some steam. Talking with Della was different than talking with Brad or her family. Della knew what life as an Agent was like, and she was also a true friend. She offered a unique and much-needed perspective.

"I could really use your advice on something," Laurel said.

"Oh? What's up?"

Laurel explained their idea about the detective agency and

her thoughts on leaving the F.B.I. Della listened intently, offering her insights and encouragement.

"You know, it's a big decision, but if anyone can make it work, it's you and your family. And if you ever need a consultant or some extra hands on a case, you know where to find me."

"You really think we can make it work?" Laurel asked. "My family has money from the apple orchards we've owned for generations, but I'm not exactly swimming in it from my government earnings. I try to stand on my own. Do you think I'd earn enough as a P.I. to support myself?"

"The truth is, the Bureau pays more, unless you're in the top tier of earners as a private investigator. People don't go into that line of work for the money," Della explained.

"Right."

"An agency is a little different, though. If you, Mikey, and your dad form a company that offers a variety of investigative services, you could see higher earnings. Especially if those services include the expertise Mikey is known for. Cybersecurity consulting and digital forensics, for instance, are in high demand. Ballparking it, I'd say your agency could earn a few million per year. You'd probably reach the low seven figures in revenue without much trouble. The great part about those investigative offerings is that they can be conducted from anywhere. You don't have to be based in a big city to make big-city money. Want me to ask around?"

"Would you?" Laurel asked.

"Sure thing," Della replied. "Maybe I can find some similar agencies for you to model after. Send me more information about your plans, when you have a chance."

Laurel breathed a sigh of relief. "That makes me feel so

much better about the whole thing," she said. "Thank you, my friend. It means a lot. By the way, if you're not busy, we could use some extra expertise on this case we're working on right now."

"You mean the woman's body that was found mutilated near your hometown?" Della asked.

"That's the one," Laurel replied. "It has me shaken up. I guess because I'm pregnant, too, and because the woman's sister is a new friend of mine. I won't be fully briefed until I get home and sit down with Jimmy—either Wednesday night or Thursday morning."

"I heard about Jimmy and his pressing need to get to Antigua," Della said with a laugh. "Some people!"

"I know, right?"

The friends laughed together. It felt good.

"If you need me, consider it done," Della said with a chuckle. "Say the word, and I'll hop on the next flight out. I can even make you some of my famous empanadas while I'm in town."

"That sounds positively heavenly," Laurel replied. "Yum."

As the conversation came to a close, Laurel could tell that Della had more on her mind.

"I know you have something else to say," Laurel said. "Out with it."

Della chuckled. "You know me. It's nothing, really. I'm just wondering if you and Brad are in a good place. I remember what torment you went through when you had broken up with him and then found out you were pregnant."

"That was a tough time, for sure," Laurel replied, twisting the hem on her shirt absentmindedly.

"I guess I wouldn't want you to be with him only because you two are having a baby," Della said. "People raise babies without being romantically involved with each other, you know? You aren't stuck. Your options are wide open."

Laurel bristled at her friend's comments, although she didn't dismiss them entirely. She loved Brad with all of her heart, but she couldn't help but wonder sometimes whether they'd be together if they weren't expecting a baby. Would she have chosen a different path? Fallen in love with a different man?

"Laurel, are you still there?" Della asked when her friend remained silent for too long.

"I'm here," she said. "It's all good. Brad and I are good. Don't worry about me, okay?"

"Easier said than done, but okay," Della replied.

As Laurel hung up, she felt lighter, despite the doubts her friend had about Brad. Talking to Della was exactly what she'd needed.

She locked her phone, then stepped inside and returned to the dining table.

Brad smiled, seeing how the tension had drained from Laurel's face. "Feel better?" he asked.

She grabbed a bottle of water from the fridge, then settled into a chair beside him. "I do feel better. Thanks for noticing."

The light from the overhead chandelier cast a warm glow over the table, softening the edges of their faces but doing little to ease the tension in the room. Laurel, Brad, Mikey, and Cornelius were about to have the first-ever meeting of their new family task force. It was a big deal.

Laurel set her water bottle down and took a deep breath.

"Okay, let's get started. We've got a lot to cover, and I don't want any surprises. Should we order food?"

Brad nodded. "Sure. Pizza sounds good. And agreed. We've got a lot of moving parts here. But first, I think there's something we need to discuss."

Cornelius looked up, his eyes meeting Brad's briefly before darting away. Mikey shifted uncomfortably in his seat. Laurel noticed the exchange, and it made her suspicious.

"What's going on?" she asked, her eyes narrowing. "What do we need to discuss?"

Brad sighed, running a hand through his hair. "It's about Jamie."

Laurel's heart skipped a beat. She'd known something was coming related to the troublesome girl, and she assumed it wasn't anything good. She suddenly felt like a cornered animal. She didn't like it one bit.

"What about her?" she asked.

Brad took a deep breath. "There's no easy way to break this news, so I'm just going to do it. You'd find out from Jimmy, anyway, and I'd rather it came from me."

"Okay."

"Jamie is pregnant, Laurel. That's why she's been staying in my carriage house. She needed a place to stay, and I offered her one."

Laurel's eyes widened in shock. "Pregnant? And you didn't think to tell me this earlier?"

Laurel quickly did the math in her head. If Brad had impregnated Jamie when they'd slept together before he had reunited with Laurel, she should be showing by now.

"But she isn't showing," Laurel said, her blood beginning to boil.

Did that mean Brad had been unfaithful since they'd been back together? Since they'd been engaged? Laurel felt foolish. And naive.

"The last time you saw her, she was wearing a big coat," Brad said. "I assure you, she's showing."

On one hand, that made Laurel feel better about the timing of things. On the other, she wondered how Brad was so certain that Jamie was showing. Had he seen her body, up close and personal? Laurel was becoming skeptical of every word out of her fiancé's mouth.

Mikey jumped in, trying to defuse the situation. "Sis, we were trying to protect you. We didn't want to add to your stress."

Laurel's gaze snapped to Mikey, then back to Brad. "Is it your baby, Brad? Is that why she's staying with you?"

Brad shook his head vehemently. "No, it's not mine. I'm just helping her out."

Laurel wasn't sure she believed him. Her mind raced as she pieced together the clues.

"What does Jimmy have to do with any of this?" she asked. "Why would I have found out from him?"

Brad sighed, shoving a hand through his hair again. "Jamie was attacked this afternoon in Appleman's Gap. I got word from Detective Nolan while you were on the porch talking to Della."

Laurel crossed her arms over her chest, huffing in response to Josh Nolan's name. He didn't seem to like her, and he was probably enjoying the fact that a love child was complicating her life.

"You *are* going to ask if she's okay, right, Sis?" Mikey asked.

"Is she okay?"

"Banged up, but yes," Brad replied. "She and the baby are fine."

Cornelius shifted again, his discomfort palpable. Laurel's eyes narrowed on him. "Dad, why do you look so guilty? Do you know something you're not telling me?"

The room fell silent. Cornelius sighed deeply, rubbing his temples. "Laurel, it's complicated."

Fourteen

LAUREL WAS FURIOUS WITH BRAD. With Mikey. With her dad.

Had they all been in on it? All hiding things from her under the guise of protecting her? Why did they think she was so fragile?

She was glad to be going back to work with the F.B.I. At least, there, she'd be respected and treated like a competent professional. Although, Jimmy had hidden things from her, too. He'd known that Jasper was her dad's grandson, yet he hadn't let her in on the secret. Was he hiding more?

She leaned back in her chair and gently tapped her temples. As she continued to tap, she moved her fingers down to the sides of her eyes, then under her eyes, under her nose, and finally to her chin. She took slow, deep breaths, trying to calm the storm of emotions swirling inside her.

Brad, watching from across the table, furrowed his brow. "Laurel, what are you doing?"

Laurel didn't stop her tapping but glanced at Brad. "It's called EFT tapping. Emotional Freedom Techniques. Della taught me how to do it. It's supposed to help with stress and anxiety."

Brad and Mikey exchanged a glance that annoyed Laurel when she saw it. They thought she was being dramatic. Little did they know that she was working hard to contain the rage bubbling just under the surface of her emotions. Stresses and disappointments had been adding up, building to a level that wasn't good for her or the baby.

Thinking about her baby wasn't so pleasant anymore. Would Jamie's baby be born around the same time? Would Laurel and Brad's baby have a sibling that wasn't Laurel's own biological child? That's not how she wanted her baby's life to be. She herself had a sibling around the same age in Sarah, yet she hadn't known about the familial connection until recently. She guessed that knowing from the beginning would be better. That was little consolation.

Brad reached out and took Laurel's hand. She let him, but warily.

"What's going on in that pretty head of yours?" he asked. "I know the news about Jamie's pregnancy came as a surprise. I'm sorry you had to find out this way."

"Is there a better way to find out that your fiancé fathered a child with a young slut?"

Brad recoiled. "Whoa, Laurel, that's not fair. I told you. I am not her baby's father."

He didn't say she wasn't a slut.

"Sure. Like how Dad wasn't Sarah's father," she said, glancing at Cornelius.

Cornelius looked down at his hands, his face filled with guilt and regret. The room fell silent, the weight of Laurel's words hanging in the air. Mikey shifted uncomfortably in his seat, his eyes darting between his sister and his father.

"Laurel," Brad began softly, "I swear to you, I have never cheated on you. I was trying to help Jamie because she needed a place to stay. That's all there is to it."

Laurel pulled her hand away from Brad's grasp, her eyes narrowing. "And you thought keeping this from me was helping? How is lying to me supposed to protect me?"

Brad sighed, running a hand through his hair. "I didn't lie to you. I didn't want to add more stress to your life. I thought we could handle this without involving you."

"Mikey leaned forward, his voice gentle but firm. "Come on, Sis, we all make mistakes. Brad was trying to do the right thing, even if it didn't come across that way."

Laurel looked at her brother, her eyes flashing with anger and hurt. "You knew about this too, Mikey? And you didn't tell me?"

Mikey nodded, his expression pained. "Yeah, I knew. But I trusted Brad to handle it. I didn't want to cause more tension between you two. You had recently gotten back together, and you're having a baby, for Pete's sake. You need to be building a family and a happy home, not being torn apart at the seams by foolishness that, ultimately, doesn't have anything to do with you."

Laurel's shoulders sagged, the fight momentarily leaving her. She felt exhausted, emotionally and physically.

"I just can't believe you all thought keeping this from me was the best option," she said. "Especially after the thing with Sarah and Jasper. I'm still not over that. I'm pretty sure I lost my best friend. Maybe I will have gained a sister, by the time it's all over. That remains to be seen. Not to mention, Mom has been put through the wringer. She's devastated. I can't help but think the whole Mack Roberts thing is a knee-jerk reaction to having been betrayed and embarrassed. So, forgive me if I'm touchy about the men in my life fathering miscellaneous children."

Cornelius finally spoke, his voice low and filled with remorse. "Laurel, I'm sorry. I've made some poor choices. I'm only human. But we need to stick together—especially now."

"Stick together? You're serious?"

"Yes, I am," Cornelius said. "We should be talking about the investigation. The news that Jamie was attacked is a significant development."

He was right.

Laurel sighed, looking around the table at the faces of the people she loved most. She could see the regret and concern etched into their features. Despite her anger, she knew they were trying their best.

"Fine," she said quietly. "But no more secrets. Agreed? I want you to be an open book. I'll give you the same courtesy in return. I don't want to have to say this ever again."

Brad, Mikey, and Cornelius all nodded in unison, their relief palpable.

Laurel took a moment to collect herself, then leaned forward and turned on her Agent Dane persona. It was time to get serious. "Okay, what do we know?" she asked.

"Let me grab my laptop to take notes," Mikey said, standing and shuffling off to the bedroom. He returned quickly with his laptop, a pen, and a pad of paper in hand.

"Good man," Brad said.

Cornelius winked at his son.

All of the men seemed happy to focus on the task at hand.

They preferred taking action as opposed to talking about feelings. Sometimes, Laurel did, too. The group shared an unspoken agreement that there had been too much emotion for one day. Anything else touchy-feely would need to wait.

"Let's begin with the most pressing case," Laurel said. "Priority number one is finding Tiana's baby."

"And hopefully, bringing her killer to justice," Brad added.

"Absolutely," Mikey agreed. "That scum needs to be taken off the streets. If you ask me, I don't much care whether that's accomplished by putting him behind bars or ... ending him."

"Ending him?" Laurel asked.

"I said what I said."

Laurel shrugged. "I get it. I'm sure Paul Douglas would agree. I can't imagine what he's going through."

"Me neither," Brad said. "Losing your wife and knowing how viciously she was killed, then knowing that your baby is missing. That your child entered the world by being cut from your wife's womb. It's unspeakable. Unthinkable."

Cornelius looked pensive. "I can confirm that having your child kidnapped is one of the most horrific experiences this world has to offer. That's why I've gone to such great lengths to bring The Cradler down. I wouldn't wish the experience on my worst enemy."

He looked at Laurel. They hadn't discussed her childhood trauma yet. She wasn't ready. Her dad was feeling her out, trying to determine where her mind was at.

"It's bad, for sure," she said. "I can only imagine. Do we have any clues? It seems likely that this was connected to The Cradler's syndicate, but it seems unlikely that he would have been the one holding the knife. I don't think he likes to get his hands dirty."

"I agree," Cornelius replied. "He has a crew of henchmen who do his dirty work for him. He's sitting back somewhere comfortable and giving orders. I'm not sure he even sees the babies he's had taken."

"That's sick," Mikey said. As a dad himself, Mikey was prone to getting very upset about this whole situation.

"So, Dad, if it isn't The Cradler himself doing the deed, how do we find the person responsible?" Laurel asked. "The Cradler is the big fish. The ultimate catch. But we might have to catch a few minnows before we can take down the boss."

"Same as with any other investigation," Cornelius said. "I'll be honest with you. I'm after The Cradler. I want to cut the head off the snake. I think that's the best way to end this reign of terror, once and for all."

"Of course, it is," Laurel said, "but my job at the Bureau has tasked me with finding Tiana's baby before anything else. Once that little one is home safe in their father's arms, I can think about the bigger picture."

"I get it," Brad said. "We're law enforcement. We work cases. Big picture has to wait sometimes."

They looked at Mikey to weigh in. "I see both points of view," he said. "Just tell me how I can help."

As the evening wore on, Laurel, Brad, Mikey, and Cornelius combed through all the evidence that they knew about, discussing likely scenarios that would lead them to answers. They solidified their commitment to share information and support each other in their common goals.

They ordered pizza and ate while they worked. Laurel wouldn't normally have indulged in that kind of food, but after the few days she'd had, she decided to splurge. Lilly appreciated the crusts that were tossed her way.

When they broke for the night, they all headed off to bed, promising to keep each other closely informed as the situation developed.

"Am I okay?" Laurel asked as she lay in bed, Brad's warm body curled around hers.

It was a silly question, on the surface, but in reality, it had great depth and meaning.

"What do you mean?" Brad asked, moving a hand under her nightshirt and finding the soft space between her breasts. "Of course, you're okay. Is your head hurting from being hit the other day?"

She shook her no. "Nothing like that. I mean in general. In life. Am I okay?"

She needed his reassurance. She might have been strong and determined at work, but in her personal life, she needed Brad to anchor her. She needed him to help her feel safe. Having been attacked again only made that desire stronger.

Finally understanding what she was asking, Brad tightened his hold on Laurel, pulling her tightly against him. His arms made a cocoon around her. Inside his protective embrace, it felt like nothing from the outside world could do her harm.

"Yes, my love," Brad said, emphasizing each word. "I promise you with everything that I am. You are okay. I'd give my life to keep you that way."

Fifteen

THE FIRST MORNING back in Appleman's Gap was a cold one. It was a stark contrast to the temperatures enjoyed on the coast. They'd been spoiled.

"Back to reality, huh?" Brad asked as he stepped out onto the front porch with a warm mug of tea in his hand. "Just the way you like it, babe, with almond milk and a dash of sugar."

Laurel had been chatting with the F.B.I. agent now stationed outside of their home, but she stopped and turned her attention to Brad. She was in Agent Dane mode, and he could tell. She was already dressed in a fitted dark pantsuit and a crisp pink blouse, her badge displayed prominently on her belt. Her growing baby bump, now visible for everyone to see, made Brad proud of his handiwork.

"Brad, meet Carter Herrington," she said as the man dutifully extended his hand. "He's day shift."

Carter looked every bit the part of a tough field Agent with a dark suit, dark sunglasses, and a don't-mess-with-me attitude.

"Morning," Brad said.

"Morning, sir," Carter said as he shook Brad's hand then resumed a pose that was reminiscent of a soldier at parade rest.

There was anticipation in the air. Laurel was going back to work, and she was ready to get things done. Lilly seemed uneasy with the energy. She whined softly at Laurel's feet. Brad gave the pup an encouraging glance.

"Are you ready to go?" Laurel asked Brad, lifting a wrist to check her watch. "I want to get to the station before Jimmy does. "I'll put my tea in a cup with a lid and take it with me."

"After you," Brad said cheerfully.

Laurel had sold her car to Dale, the cook from Jack and Jill's, and she hadn't replaced it yet because she had access to Brad's truck when he drove his police cruiser. He'd left the cruiser at the station while they were out of town, though, which meant that they were riding to the station together today.

When they arrived, Jimmy was already there, sitting at one of the big conference tables with his laptop open and files spread out in front of him. He looked up as they entered, his expression serious but warm.

"Morning, you two," Jimmy greeted. "I wish we were meeting under better circumstances."

Laurel nodded, taking a seat. "At least, you're heading to Antigua when this meeting is over."

"Lucky dog, you," Brad said with a smile.

"What's the latest?" Laurel asked.

Jimmy sighed, closing his laptop. "I have some updates for you before I head back to D.C. and then off to the island for the family wedding. I wanted to make sure you're fully briefed on the situation. Are you ready to take over, Laurel?"

She nodded. "I'm ready."

Brad leaned forward, his attention fully on Jimmy. "What do we know about the attack on Jamie?"

Jimmy handed Laurel a folder.

"Jamie was attacked in the parking lot of a nail salon on Broad Street. We have reason to believe it wasn't random. The Cradler left a note addressed to you, Laurel. He's warning you to back off. He says he almost had you at the park in Mount Pleasant, and that next time, he won't miss."

Laurel opened the folder and read the note, her anger flaring. "We're not backing off. We're going to find him and bring him down."

Jimmy nodded. "I expected as much. But there's more. We've identified a new player in The Cradler's operation. Someone who does the dirty work in cases like Tiana's."

Laurel's brow furrowed. "Who?"

"A man known as The Dark Hand," Jimmy said, his tone grave. "He's been linked to several similar cases. We believe he's the one who took Tiana's baby and attacked Jamie."

"Is he the same one who came after me? Or Dad?"

"No," Jimmy replied. "That was another henchman. Two others, actually. We don't have a positive ID on either yet."

Brad clenched his fists. "Well, we know about The Dark Hand. We need to find him. Fast."

Jimmy looked at them both, his expression intense. "We have a lead on his location. But you need to be careful. This guy is dangerous. Brad, I've already coordinated with your team, but I asked them to wait for your go-ahead. I'm leaving the rest to the two of you."

"That's awfully cooperative of you, Jimmy," Brad said

with a smirk. "I thought you Bureau people didn't like to play nice with us small-town police departments."

Jimmy chuckled. "For you, Chief Tate, I'll make an exception."

Laurel interjected, "What about Tiana's baby? Do we have any updates on him or her?"

Jimmy's face grew even more serious. "Her. Forensics confirmed that Tiana had a baby girl."

Laurel closed her eyes for a few seconds. She hadn't told anyone, but she'd been predicting that her own baby was a girl. They could find out at her upcoming OB appointment, if they wanted to. The fact that Tiana had a baby girl made the case hit even harder.

"Okay," Brad said.

"We've been working around the clock trying to find her," Jimmy explained. "We believe The Dark Hand has the baby, and our intel suggests she's still alive. There's a strong possibility that The Dark Hand is keeping her as leverage. Our top priority is to find her and bring her back safely."

"Has there been a ransom demand?" Laurel asked.

"No."

"The bastard."

Laurel took a deep breath, feeling the weight of the responsibility. "Let's get this done. We need to find The Dark Hand and rescue that baby."

Jimmy nodded. "I've arranged for additional support from the Bureau. Agents will be arriving throughout the day to assist in the search and provide any backup you need."

"More agents?" Laurel asked. "Not just Samira and Malik. What changed?"

Jimmy sighed, then looked Laurel straight in the eye.

"We have evidence to believe that a case out in California is connected to The Cradler. In a quiet, wine-country town called Rosemary Run, a baby was cut out of its mother's womb. As far as the Bureau is concerned, it's time for all hands on deck. They're devoting the necessary resources."

"Wow. This is nationwide," Brad said, leaning back in his chair.

He was out of his depth, and he knew it. Meanwhile, Laurel seemed to take the news in stride. This marked the difference between life as a police officer and life as an F.B.I. agent.

""Thank you, Jimmy. We'll take it from here," Laurel said. "I've got this."

Jimmy stood, gathering his files. "I have to get going. But I'll be in touch. And remember, you have the full support of the Bureau behind you."

Laurel stood and hugged Jimmy. "Safe travels. And thank you for everything."

Jimmy nodded, giving Brad a firm handshake. "Take care of each other. And bring this bastard down."

They confirmed that they absolutely would.

As Jimmy turned to go, Laurel grabbed his arm. "Wait. What about my dad?"

"He'll be brought to the nearby safe house later today. You'll be kept informed, but I can't express enough how careful you need to be. Your dad is supposed to be a dead man. If he screws this up, he will become one, for real. There's already a credible threat to his cover."

"I understand," Laurel replied.

"Does he know?" Brad asked.

Jimmy nodded. "He's been made aware, although he doesn't know the identity of the informant. Not officially."

"Got it," Brad replied.

"Hey, Della has agreed to run point on this from D.C.," Jimmy said to Laurel. "I thought it might help to have a friend on the other end of the line when you call for help. You *will* end up calling for help. There's no shame in that."

"I understand."

Just as Jimmy turned to leave, the door swung open, and Detective Josh Nolan strode in, his expression as cold as the morning air outside. He glanced around the room, his eyes landing on Laurel with an unmistakable hostility.

"Morning," Josh said curtly, acknowledging Jimmy and Brad with a brief nod before fixing his glare on Laurel. His jet-black hair was freshly slicked back, making his appearance harsh. "Agent Dane, I need a word."

Laurel squared her shoulders, meeting his gaze head-on. "Go ahead, Detective. We're all ears."

Josh scoffed, crossing his arms over his chest. "You've brought a lot of trouble to our town, Agent Dane. Ever since you showed up, it's been one disaster after another. First, we have Jasper Hobbs' kidnapping, then Tiana Sneed's murder and the kidnapping of her unborn child, and now the attack on Jamie Beck. And let's not forget the chaos at the fish fry."

Laurel's jaw tightened. "He knows ... about my dad?" she asked Jimmy.

"It's my job to know," Josh said before Jimmy had a chance to answer. "We have to hide him, somehow."

"I'm aware of the risks, Detective," Laurel said. "We're doing everything we can to bring these criminals to justice."

Josh shook his head, a sneer forming on his lips. "Justice?

What about the safety of our town? Appleman's Gap was a quiet, safe place before you turned it into a crime scene. Your presence here is a liability, not an asset."

Brad stepped forward, his voice low and menacing. "Watch your tone, Nolan. Agent Dane is here to help. We're all working together to solve this."

Josh ignored Brad, his focus still on Laurel. "And your father, the so-called hero of Appleman's Gap. Look at the mess he's left behind. His legacy is nothing but a stain on this town now."

Laurel's fists clenched at her sides. "You have no right to insult my father. He dedicated his life to this community. Just because things have gotten complicated doesn't mean his legacy is tarnished."

Josh's eyes flashed with anger. "Complicated? People are dying, Agent Dane. And you're bringing more danger with you. If it were up to me, you and your father would be kept far away from here."

Brad couldn't hold back any longer. He stepped closer to Nolan, his voice a low growl. "That's enough, Nolan. Laurel is doing her job, and she's damn good at it. If you have a problem with that, take it up with me. Must I remind you of the chain of command?"

Josh took a step back, clearly rattled by Brad's intensity. He glanced at Jimmy, who watched the exchange with a neutral expression.

Jimmy finally spoke, his tone calm but authoritative. "Detective Nolan, I understand your concerns, but we're all on the same side here. The Bureau is fully committed to finding Tiana's baby and bringing The Dark Hand to justice. We need to work together."

Nolan huffed but seemed to concede, albeit reluctantly. "Fine. But I'm watching you, Agent Dane. One more slip-up, and I'll make sure you're off this case."

Laurel nodded, her voice steady despite the anger simmering beneath the surface. "Understood, Detective."

Josh turned on his heel and stormed out of the room, leaving a tense silence in his wake.

Sixteen

CORNELIUS DANE STRETCHED and wiped the sleep from his eyes, a warm mug of coffee in one hand as he stood on the back deck of his newest safe house.

This time, it was freezing cold. Seneca Lake, New York provided gorgeous views, but the temperatures left much to be desired. A fresh blanket of snow had fallen since Cornelius had arrived the night before, and there was at least six inches of it still on the ground.

"Well, Sully boy," he said to his imaginary dog, "so much for Jimmy liking the beach. I suppose he likes the water, since well, here we are." He gestured to the lake in front of him. "But this isn't what I had in mind when I complimented his tastes a few days ago from the comfort of the Carolinas."

Watkins Glen was a tiny town at the southernmost end of Seneca Lake. It was Cornelius' temporary home until the safe house near Appleman's Gap was ready.

Cornelius had been told there were pretty waterfalls and gorges in the area, but he wouldn't have the luxury of exploring any of them. He was under strict instructions to stay indoors and out of sight. He probably shouldn't have been out on the deck right now, but he desperately needed some mental stimulation.

He could see the Watkins Glen Marina pier from here. At the end of the pier, a wooden structure with red shake shingles housed a blue sign that read "Seneca Lake." A few lonely boats sat in their slips at the adjacent marina, covered in snow and ice. Cornelius figured many boats had been moved for the winter. Although, he was no expert on such matters and didn't know for sure.

He'd been instructed to change his appearance again. The first order of business was shaving his scraggly beard, which Cornelius looked forward to. He stepped inside, closing and locking the sliding glass door, then headed for the bathroom and a shiny, fresh razor that had been left for him.

"Time to go bye bye, beard," he said as he lathered shaving cream on his face and began the delicate process.

When he was finished with that task, he moved on to the box of hair dye that sat waiting on the side of the tub.

The pictures on the insert touted an easy way to permanently cover gray. Cornelius wasn't so sure, though. He'd had gray hair for more than two decades that had never been colored. He couldn't imagine that a bottle of dye could change his look all that much.

As he applied the dye, his new phone buzzed on the counter. Just as before, only a few people had the number. Cornelius glanced at the screen and saw a message from Jimmy.

All clear. Stay put and stay safe. I'm out for
the rest of the week. Your daughter has
things under control.

Cornelius sighed, feeling a mix of frustration and relief. He rinsed out the dye, toweling his hair dry, and was surprised to see a younger-looking version of himself staring back from the mirror. The dark brown color had indeed made a significant difference.

He decided to explore the safe house a bit more. The living room was cozy, with a large fireplace that looked inviting. Cornelius gathered some wood and kindling, deciding to start a fire. As the flames crackled to life, he felt a small sense of accomplishment.

Next, he headed to the kitchen. The agents who had set up the safe house had brought some basic supplies, and the pantry was stocked with various non-perishable items. Cornelius decided to try his hand at baking bread, something he hadn't done in years. He found a simple recipe in one of the cookbooks on the shelf and got to work, kneading the dough and setting it aside to rise.

While waiting for the dough, he settled on the couch with a book he found on the shelf, an old mystery novel that he remembered enjoying years ago. As he read, the scent of baking bread began to fill the house, giving it a warm, comforting atmosphere.

Hours passed quietly, and Cornelius found himself feeling more at peace. The bread turned out well, and he enjoyed a slice with some butter, savoring the simple pleasure.

After cleaning up the kitchen, he decided it was time to get back to work. Cornelius made his way to the small office that had been set up for him. The room was functional, with a sturdy desk, a comfortable chair, and a laptop with a secure connection to the Bureau's network.

He logged in and started reviewing the latest updates on The Cradler case. He read through reports, analyzed data, and coordinated with his contacts. Every piece of information brought them closer to dismantling the syndicate and ensuring the safety of his family.

Cornelius' phone buzzed again, this time with a secure message from Laurel. It contained details about a recent sighting of The Dark Hand, the new player they had identified. Cornelius's eyes narrowed as he read through the intel, feeling a surge of determination.

He spent the next few hours mapping out potential locations and identifying weaknesses in The Cradler's operation. He sent encrypted messages to Laurel and Brad, updating them on his findings and suggesting strategies for their next move. He wasn't sure if he was actually helping, but it felt good to be connected in some small way.

As Cornelius worked, the scent of the freshly baked bread lingered in the air, a reminder of the simple, human pleasures that balanced the tension of his dangerous lifestyle. He stepped back onto the deck, the cold air biting at his skin, and looked out over the frozen lake.

"We're going to get them, Sully," he said quietly to his imaginary companion. "We're going to bring them all down, and we're going to keep our family safe. Then I can stop hiding. You can join me in real life."

As he stood there, a sense of loneliness crept in.

He missed Maureen. She would have eaten freshly-baked bread with him, and she would have enjoyed it thoroughly.

He missed the way she used to laugh at his silly jokes, the way she would fuss over him when he was being stubborn, and the warmth of her presence. Truth be told, Carmen and Tricia were merely distractions. They were Cornelius' attempt to avoid admitting that he missed his wife. He was devastated that she'd taken up with Mack Roberts.

He longed to hear Maureen's voice, to tell her everything that was happening, but he knew it was too dangerous.

He thought about Jamie. She was young and scared, and she had been thrust into a situation she never asked for. Cornelius felt a protective instinct toward her, a need to make sure she was okay. He knew he needed to reach out to her, to let her know she wasn't alone.

He decided to use a more discreet method to contact her. Remembering that younger people often used encrypted messaging apps for privacy, he decided to download one. He set up an account with a pseudonym and sent Jamie a message.

> Hey Jamie, don't use my name, but it's …
> daddy. Catch my drift? Just checking in to
> see how you're holding up. If you need
> anything, let me know. Stay safe.

Jamie's father was a bum living on unemployment in a trailer park in Mississsppi. He couldn't afford a phone or computer, let alone figure out how to message her through one. She knew exactly who this was.

Cornelius waited, the minutes stretching out as he stared at the screen. Finally, a reply came.

> Hi. I'm okay, just really scared. Thank you for reaching out. It means a lot. How are you?

He smiled, feeling a bit of the weight lift from his shoulders. He typed back.

> Taking it one day at a time. Remember, you're not alone in this. If you ever need to talk, I'm just a message away.

They exchanged a few more messages, the conversation light and supportive. Cornelius could sense Jamie's relief in her words, and it made him feel better knowing he was providing some comfort. He logged off the app, feeling a bit more connected to the world.

"Becoming a dad again at my age wasn't in the plan, Sully," Cornelius said out loud. "What am I going to do?"

Laurel was liable to kill him when she found out, he knew that much. Although, she'd be relieved that Brad wasn't the baby's father. The timing of everything could only be described as comical.

Cornelius and Jamie had slept together a few weeks prior to Brad arriving in Appleman's Gap. They'd met at Gap Grounds Coffee Co. the summer before and had stayed in touch. Jamie had been working there, and Cornelius had frequented the spot for morning coffee and donuts. When Cornelius had faked his death and suddenly had no friends or family to talk to, he had confided in Jamie, figuring she wouldn't blow his cover because she was too young and naive to do so. They became close, which ultimately led to a romantic relationship. Cornelius knew better, but he was lonely and desperate. Not to mention, beautiful women were his weakness.

When Jamie and Brad met at the same coffee shop in town a few weeks later, she had just found out she was pregnant.

Assuming that Cornelius—technically a dead man—wouldn't step up to help her raise the child, she was in the mood to act out. Enter Brad, who was missing Laurel and their life in Washington, D.C. Against his better judgement, he'd allowed himself to be seduced by the pretty young woman. Brad had put a swift end to it, though, only sleeping with Jamie once. Imagine his surprise when he found out that Cornelius had gotten her pregnant. Cornelius needed a place for Jamie to live while he sorted out his situation and determined how to best support his baby.

Even in a small town like Appleman's Gap, a young, single woman would have a near-impossible time supporting a child on a coffee shop salary.

"Laurel will come around, eventually," Cornelius said to the imaginary Sully. "Maureen, on the other hand, might not."

Seventeen

KANESHA WAS in tears when she burst through the doors of the station.

It reminded Laurel of the night of the carjacking, when she herself had arrived shaken and distraught. That memory swirled with childhood ones of visiting her dad here. The place was one of heightened emotion, for many of the people who came through its doors.

"I need to speak to Laurel," Kanesha said to Matt Wilson at the front desk. "Agent Laurel Dane. She knows me."

Laurel had seen her friend park and walk inside. She arrived in the lobby just as Matt offered Kanesha a fresh tissue to dry her eyes. It was a good guess on Kanesha's part to think that Laurel would be here. With no F.B.I. offices in Appleman's Gap, the police station was the next best option for setting up a homebase.

"Kanesha," Laurel called gently.

Kanesha turned, her face pained by grief and desperation. "Laurel! Oh, thank God. I didn't know who else to turn to."

Laurel wrapped her arms around Kanesha in a comforting embrace. "I'm here. Come on, let's go to the conference room where we can talk in private. I'm using it as a temporary office."

She led Kanesha down the hall, away from the bustling lobby, and into a quiet room. Brad and Laurel exchanged concerned glances, but he gave the women their space.

Once they were seated, Kanesha broke down again. "Laurel, what am I supposed to do? Paul refuses to eat. He's just sitting there, staring at the wall in my apartment. I don't know how to help him. I don't know what to do."

Laurel's heart ached for her friend. She reached across the table, taking Kanesha's hand. "We're doing everything we can to find Tiana's baby and bring her home. I promise you that. But right now, you need to take care of yourself and Paul. He needs you."

Kanesha nodded, tears streaming down her face. "I know, but it's so hard. Every time I look at him, I see Tiana. And knowing what happened to her... it's unbearable."

Laurel squeezed her hand. "I can't imagine how difficult this is for you. But you have to stay strong, for Paul and for Tiana's baby. We will find her. And we will bring the people responsible to justice."

"Her? Are you sure it's a girl?"

Laurel nodded sympathetically. "Yes, forensics confirmed her sex. You have a niece."

"Tiana would have been over the moon to have a daughter." Kanesha wiped her eyes with the tissue Matt had given her. "I just don't know how to keep going. Paul hasn't eaten in days. He's wasting away in front of me."

Laurel took a deep breath, trying to find the right words.

"Grief affects everyone differently. Maybe Paul needs professional help to get through this. A therapist or a grief counselor could make a big difference. And you, too. Don't hesitate to reach out to someone for support. My mom saw someone in town after my dad died. I can get you a name, if you like."

It felt strange for Laurel to talk about her dad this way, but she couldn't reveal the truth. Not yet.

Kanesha nodded, though she still looked lost. "That would be good. Thank you. But it feels like I'm failing him. Failing Tiana."

"You're not failing anyone," Laurel said firmly. "You're doing the best you can in an unimaginable situation. And you're not alone. We're all here for you. The whole team is working tirelessly to find Tiana's baby and to bring the criminals to justice."

Kanesha shuddered. "Thank you, Laurel. I just needed to hear that. I needed to know that someone cares. I've been out of my mind with you gone. No one has told me much."

As if on cue, Samira and Malik came through the door of the conference room, ready for their morning meeting with Laurel. They planned to touch base on the overview first, then discuss in more detail in a few hours, once Laurel had time to catch up. She nodded at them, indicating she would be just a moment longer with Kanesha.

"I care, Kanesha. We all do," Laurel said softly. "If you have any questions, now's the time to ask. I want you to feel informed and supported."

Kanesha took a deep breath, trying to steady herself. "Do you have any leads? Anything that could help us find Tiana's baby?"

Laurel exchanged a glance with Samira, who stepped forward. "I'm Agent Samira Aziz and this is my partner, Agent Malik Washington. We're actively working on it. We have identified a suspect known as The Dark Hand. He's believed to be involved in Tiana's case and several others. We're doing everything we can to track him down."

Kanesha nodded, though the information seemed to overwhelm her. "What about the local police? Are they helping?"

Malik stepped in, his voice calm and reassuring. "Yes, they're fully involved. They weren't at first, but it's all hands on deck at this point. We're working closely with Detective Nolan and his team to ensure that every lead is followed up on. Chief Tate, too, now that he's back."

Kanesha sniffled, dabbing at her eyes with the tissue. "And Paul ... what should I do about him?"

Laurel gave her friend a compassionate look. "Encourage him to see a therapist. It's not a sign of weakness to seek help. In fact, it's one of the strongest things you can do right now."

Kanesha nodded again, looking slightly more composed as her long braids danced around her shoulders. "Thank you, Laurel. I needed this. I'll talk to Paul about seeing someone."

"Is there any family who can come up from Florida to help you?" Laurel asked.

"Maybe."

"I think that would be a good idea," Laurel said. "Talk to Paul and figure out who you can ask."

Kanesha nodded.

"Oh, one more thing," Laurel said.

"Yeah?"

"Now that we know the baby is a girl, does your niece have a name?"

Kanesha smiled, her eyes momentarily bright. "Alexia. Alexia Nicole Douglas. She's named after one of our grandmothers."

"Beautiful name." Laurel squeezed her friend's hand one last time. "Take care, Kanesha. I'll be in touch soon, okay? And remember, we're just a phone call away."

Kanesha stood, giving Laurel a weak smile. "Thank you. I'll let you get back to your work."

Laurel watched Kanesha leave the room, then turned to Samira and Malik. Her face was all serious business. "Good to see you both looking well. Thank you for being here. Let's get started. What do we know so far?"

Samira pulled out her tablet, bringing up the latest reports. "We've confirmed that The Dark Hand was in the area around the time of Tiana's murder. He has a history of similar crimes, and we believe he's holding the baby as leverage."

"Leverage for what? No ransom demands have been made, correct?"

Samira shook her head. "Correct, no ransom demands. We believe he's using the baby to control someone or to ensure silence. It's possible he's waiting for the right moment to make a move or he might be waiting for further instructions from The Cradler."

Laurel frowned, absorbing the information. "So, we're dealing with a sadist who's following orders. Typical. Do we have any idea where he might be hiding?"

Malik shook his head. "Not yet, but we're following several leads. We've got surveillance on his known associates and are monitoring communications. It's only a matter of time before he slips up."

Samira continued, "We've also found some evidence linking him to a drug house in a nearby town. We're planning a raid, but we need to be sure the baby is there before we move in."

Laurel leaned forward, her mind racing. "Is Detective Nolan cooperating?"

Malik exchanged a look with Samira. "He's ... reluctant. He doesn't like the idea of federal agents taking over his investigation, but he's providing us with the necessary resources."

"That's about what I expected. We'll have to work around him if necessary. The guy seems to have a beef with me. I have no idea why. I'm sorry that it's affecting you."

"It's okay," Malik said, his brown skin and strong features pleasing to Laurel's eye.

She'd thought he was an incredibly handsome man when they'd met, and she still admired his good looks. He seemed like a truly decent guy, too, if a little young for her. Focusing on the task at hand, she pushed those thoughts aside. She was happy with Brad, anyway. Wasn't she?

"What's our next move?" Laurel asked.

"You tell us, boss," Malik said.

"No, you two have been on the ground, involved in this investigation for nearly a week," Laurel replied. "I appreciate your insight. You tell me."

Laurel always enjoyed mentoring younger agents. It had become one of her favorite parts of the job.

Bolstered by the vote of confidence, Samira pulled up a map on her tablet, showing various locations of interest. "We continue the surveillance and try to narrow down The Dark Hand's location. We'll coordinate with local law enforcement for the raid, but we need to move quickly. The longer he has the baby, the more dangerous the situation becomes."

"Do we have an ID on this guy other than The Dark Hand? I presume his momma didn't name him that," Laurel said.

"Not yet," Malik replied. "DNA found at the scene didn't match anything in our database."

Laurel sighed, leaning back in her chair. "Alright, we need to get a positive ID on this guy. Let's focus on gathering more intel and putting pressure on his associates. Someone's bound to crack."

Samira nodded, scrolling through her notes. "We have a few leads on potential associates who might know something. We've been monitoring their communications, and one of them has been acting nervous. He could be our way in."

Laurel leaned forward, her eyes sharp. "Who is he?"

"Jerome Swenson," Samira replied. "Small-time crook with ties to The Cradler's operation. He's been seen frequenting a bar downtown. We're planning to bring him in for questioning."

Laurel nodded, her mind buzzing with possibilities. "Good. Let's make sure we handle this delicately. We don't want to spook him or anyone else in The Cradler's circle."

Malik added, "We'll set up surveillance at the bar and track his movements. If he leads us to The Dark Hand, we can make our move."

Laurel stood. "All right, let's get to work. Samira, coordinate with Detective Nolan and set up the surveillance. Malik, keep monitoring the communications. I'll reach out to our informants and see if we can get any additional information. Stay close. We'll reconvene in a few hours, when I've had a chance to comb through the case file. I'll ask for crime scene details then. Be ready to report."

Samira and Malik nodded, gathering their equipment and heading out to execute their plan. Laurel watched them go, feeling a mix of pride and anxiety. They had a solid lead, but there was still so much that could go wrong.

Eighteen

A BLANK SHEET of white paper waited on the desk as Cornelius stared at it expectantly. With a black pen clutched firmly in hand, he intended to write a bucket list of things he wanted to do before he died.

"It's morbid, I know," he said to his imaginary dog. "Call me crazy, but I feel the need to do this. Either I'll be actually dead soon because The Cradler and his goons got me, or I will have reinvented myself and the old Cornelius will be dead. Whichever way it plays out, I figure I should get clear on what I want."

He wrote number one in big letters: Live in a warmer climate than New York. That made him laugh, which was good. He'd been taking himself too seriously.

"Really, though," he said out loud. "I could live a lot of places. The Charleston area was great. But at the end of the day, Appleman's Gap, Tennessee is my home. I want to get back there and make peace with the people I love. I can't see myself living anywhere else. So, Sully, that means you had better like swimming in the lake, hiking the hills, and hanging around my family's apple orchard. Get ready. I plan to keep you busy."

Number two came easily: Get a black lab puppy. There, he had officially claimed his desire for a canine companion. Now he wouldn't have to feel quite so foolish talking to an imaginary friend. That friend would be live and in the flesh—and fur—one day soon.

Number three was also easy to choose: Reconcile with Maureen and live as a happily married couple again. That one would be much harder to make happen. Not only had Cornelius betrayed her by faking his own death and letting her grieve, but he'd fathered a love child with Linda Peterson and another one with Jamie Beck. The fact that Jamie was twenty-three wouldn't help matters. Maureen had been publicly embarrassed when it had come out that Sarah Peterson was Cornelius' daughter, and he hadn't been there to comfort her. He could only imagine how upset she'd be when she found out about Jamie. With Mack Roberts on Maureen's arm and whispering sweet nothings in her ear, it would take a miracle for Cornelius to win her back. He intended to try his damndest.

Number four: Repair the relationship with his kids. That would take a lot of doing. He was working on it with Laurel and Mikey, but Maggie, Hazel, and Ryan needed attention, too. Not to mention, he needed to start a new father-daughter relationship with Sarah. He intended to be involved from the beginning with Jamie's baby. Regardless of how they came into this world, each of his children deserved to know a loving, available father.

Number five: Convince the townspeople of Appleman's Gap that faking his death was for a good cause and make them believe he was a good man at heart. Cornelius knew there would be misunderstandings, but he hoped that in time, his friends and neighbors in town would love him again. He had been their Chief for so long. He wanted to maintain the good reputation he had built. He wanted people to like him.

"Wow, boy," Cornelius said. "I'm only on number five and already, I'm overwhelmed. These items are no small tasks. I've really screwed up my life."

He stared at the paper for a few moments, letting the weight of his choices settle in. He knew the road ahead would be tough, but writing down his goals made them feel more tangible. More achievable. He took a deep breath and continued.

Number six: Make amends with the people I've hurt. This included more than just his family. There were friends, colleagues, and townspeople who had been affected by his decisions. He needed to face them, explain his actions, and ask for their forgiveness.

Cornelius had a hunch he knew who the informant Jimmy had mentioned was—a former colleague named Victor Garton.

Vic had been a detective in Appleman's Gap for over two decades. With Cornelius as Chief, the pair had brought dozens of criminals to justice. Vic had been there when The Cradler's father, Lucien Somerset, was terrorizing Middle Tennessee. He'd known about Laurel's kidnapping, and had helped bring her home safely.

The thought of Vic doubting him was hard for Cornelius to take, but Vic had expressed concern about Cornelius' methods on several occasions. He thought Cornelius was bending the rules too much and taking too many liberties in pursuit of Lucian and his network. It was why Vic had eventually left Tennessee and took a job at a police department in Florida. It made sense that he'd be a whistleblower, if he thought that Cornelius was up to no good.

"That's going to be a tough one," Cornelius mused. "Vic is like a dog with a bone, once he gets his mind set on something."

He moved on. Number seven: Find peace within myself. Cornelius knew that all the external changes and reconciliations would mean little if he couldn't find a way to forgive himself. He had to let go of the guilt and regret that weighed him down and learn to live with his choices.

Hopefully, he'd make better decisions in the future. No more affairs. No more love children. In fact, a vasectomy wouldn't be a bad idea.

Cornelius set the pen down, feeling a bit lighter having put his thoughts on paper. He stood up, stretched, and decided to check on the bread he had baked earlier. The scent still lingered in the air, a comforting reminder of simpler times.

As he sliced another piece and spread butter over it, he thought about Maureen again. He longed to hear her voice and to tell her everything that was happening, but he reminded himself that it was too dangerous. Instead, he decided to continue with his list, adding a few lighter goals to balance out the heavy ones. He picked up the pen again and smiled as he wrote.

Number eight: Ride a horse on a mountain trail. He had always enjoyed horseback riding, and the idea of exploring the mountains on horseback sounded like a peaceful and exhilarating experience. Ideally, this was something he and Maureen would do together, while they were still young enough to do it safely and enjoy the experience.

Number nine: Hang glide over the Smoky Mountains. Cornelius chuckled at this one. It was something he had always wanted to try, and now seemed like the perfect time to add it to his list. The thrill of soaring above the mountains would be a memory to cherish. This item seemed the most outrageous. Aside from repairing the relationships with his family, this one would certainly be the scariest. He wasn't a big fan of heights.

Number ten: Dive in tropical waters. He had never been much of a beach person, but the idea of diving into the clear, warm waters of a tropical location intrigued him. The vibrant underwater world would be a stark contrast to the cold, snowy environment he was currently in. Besides, how hard could it be? There would be a guide to help him navigate the experience, right?

Number eleven, a bonus: Publish a book of recipes. Cornelius had always enjoyed cooking, and over the years, he had collected a variety of recipes. Putting them together in a book would be a way to share his passion for food with others and leave a lasting legacy that was more enjoyable than anything he'd ever do in law enforcement.

He set the pen down once more and looked over his list. It was a mix of serious and fun, and it felt like a true reflection of the life he wanted to lead. Cornelius knew that achieving these goals would take time and effort, but for the first time in a long while, he felt a glimmer of hope for the future.

Suddenly inspired to move around, Cornelius used his

new phone to play some music. He chose "Friendship" by Chris Stapleton.

Bouncing out into the hallway, he skipped and spun, pretending that Sully was there with him. The easy strums of the guitar and Chris' raspy voice made it feel like he was back in Tennessee. Reaching the main living area where there was more open space, Cornelius closed his eyes and held his hands out down low, where Sully's paws would be. He looked ridiculous, dancing with an imaginary dog, but what did he care? No one was there to witness the spectacle.

As Chris sang about the kind of friendship to last a lifetime, Cornelius let himself feel happy and free.

Satisfied with his personal progress when the song was over, Cornelius turned his attention back to the work that needed to be done. The Cradler and his network were still out there, and he was committed to bringing them down. It wouldn't hurt his chances to please Laurel and Mikey, either, as they considered opening a detective agency with their old dad.

Returning to the computer that had been set up for him, he logged into the secure network and began reviewing the latest updates.

"We've got this, Sully," he said quietly. "We've got this."

Cornelius was immersed in his work when a sharp knock on the door pulled him back to reality. His heart rate spiked as he set the pen down and quickly stood, glancing around the room. He wasn't expecting anyone.

Before heading to the door, he walked over to a drawer in the small office. He opened it and retrieved a handgun, checking to make sure it was loaded. He tucked the gun into the back of his waistband, ensuring it was easily accessible but out of sight.

With the gun securely in place, Cornelius cautiously approached the door, peeking through the peephole, but saw no one. He slowly unlocked and opened the door, looking around the snowy yard. No footprints in the fresh snow. No signs of movement, other than a beautiful red cardinal perched on the heavy branch of an evergreen tree.

He was reminded of the heron at James Island County Park in South Carolina and the way the bird had seemed to offer its support. Even though it was silly, he felt like this red bird was willing to give him a moral boost, too. He quickly nodded his thanks.

His suspicion grew as he closed the door and bolted it. He made his way to the security console in the office, intending to review the camera feed. He pressed a few buttons, and the monitor flickered to life, but instead of showing a live feed, it displayed a blank screen with the words "Signal Lost."

"Dammit," he muttered under his breath. Whoever had knocked had also disabled the cameras. This wasn't some random act. It was someone who knew what they were doing.

Cornelius grabbed his phone and immediately sent a secure message to Jimmy's number, detailing what had just happened. Jimmy was out of town, but his messages should have been set to forward to someone.

Cornelius knew he needed to be on high alert. His safe house was compromised.

He went back to the kitchen, retrieved a knife, and tucked it into his waistband alongside the gun, feeling a familiar sense of urgency and paranoia. He couldn't shake the feeling that someone was watching him, waiting for the right moment to strike.

As he paced the living room, his mind raced with possibilities. Was it The Cradler's men? Was someone else involved? He needed to stay vigilant and prepare for the worst. Cornelius decided to do a thorough check of the house, ensuring all doors and windows were locked and secure.

When that was finished and everything checked out okay, he returned to the office and opened a secure line of communication with Laurel and Brad. They needed to be aware of the situation and take any necessary precautions. As he typed out the message, he couldn't help but feel a twinge of guilt for dragging his family into this mess. But he knew they were strong and capable. They would get through this.

Afterward, Cornelius took a deep breath and tried to calm his nerves. He couldn't afford to panic. He returned to his desk and stared at the list he had made earlier. It felt almost surreal to think about those goals now, with danger lurking just outside.

The knock on the door had shaken him, but it also reinforced his resolve. He was determined to rebuild his life and protect his family. He just needed to stay one step ahead of whoever was after him.

PART THREE

Working Together

Nineteen

AS LAUREL SAT BACK DOWN at the desk Brad had set up for her in the corner of the conference room, her phone buzzed with a message from him. It felt good to be back to work, but she was walking a fine line between the world she'd known and the one unfolding for her Brad, and their baby.

You okay?

Laurel smiled, typing a quick response.

> Yeah, just a lot on my mind. We're making progress, though. The baby's name is Alexia Nicole.

It took Brad a minute. Three dots appeared on and off as he was typing, but nothing came through for what seemed like forever.

Our baby?

> No, silly. I wouldn't name our baby without consulting you. Alexia is the name of Tiana's baby. Kanesha was here and told me.

> Good. I wasn't sure what to say, for a minute.

> We'll talk at home tonight. That is, if Jamie doesn't interrupt.

> Babe, stop it. I won't let her interfere.

Laurel set her phone aside and took a deep breath. She wasn't so sure. She couldn't think about Jamie now, though. They were making progress in the investigation, but the clock was ticking. Every moment they delayed was another moment Tiana's baby was in danger. With Jimmy away, it was on her to make things happen.

She reviewed the case files once more, making notes and formulating a plan. They needed to act fast and smart. There was no room for error.

If only the baby wasn't pressing on her bladder. At first, pregnancy hormones had kept her running to the bathroom. At this point in the pregnancy, the weight of the baby was beginning to cause more trouble. That would only get worse. It was a preview of just how much Laurel's life was going to change.

"Suck it up, Dane," Laurel said quietly to herself. "Plenty of pregnant women work."

While lounging around at home all day had been a luxury, she knew she couldn't do it forever. At least, she knew she shouldn't do it forever. People needed her. They needed the particular set of skills she possessed to investigate crimes and see that the guilty were brought to justice.

Before Laurel could get too far into the files, Samira and Malik returned. They had been part of the initial investigation into Tiana Douglas' murder, and she needed to be brought up to speed on the details of exactly what had happened the day Tiana's body was found and processed.

This was the nitty gritty stuff. The stuff that Laurel had less of a stomach for, now that she was pregnant. It had to be covered, though.

Malik had attended University of Tennessee, Knoxville, where he'd studied forensics at the Body Farm. Even though he was a young agent without a lot of field experience, he was well qualified.

"Welcome back," Laurel said to the agents. "Thank you for giving me time to look over the files."

They nodded and smiled.

Laurel hoped that her demeanor was friendlier than Jimmy's. Maybe it was a result of having been raised in the South. Whatever the origin, she figured that Samira and Malik appreciated it. Jimmy was a good guy at heart, but he could be exhausting—especially during the middle of a tense investigation.

Samira pulled out her tablet, bringing up the latest reports and images from the crime scene. She was all business.

"All right, Laurel, here's what happened," she said. "When we first arrived at the scene, it was clear that this was a highly organized and premeditated crime."

Malik nodded, taking over.

"The body was found in a remote section near the edge of the forest in the area known as Cedar Hollow, about ten miles outside of Appleman's Gap. She was lying on a bed of leaves, and it was evident that she had been placed there postmortem. There were no signs of a struggle at the location, indicating she was likely killed elsewhere and transported."

Laurel's expression remained stern as she absorbed the information. "What about the initial examination of the body?"

Samira tapped her tablet, bringing up images of the forensic examination.

Laurel found herself wanting to look away, but she took a breath and forced her eyes to do their part. She wasn't a kid anymore. She couldn't cover her eyes and bury her head in her dad's strong embrace because a scary part of a movie had come on. This was real life. This was her job.

"Tiana's cause of death was exsanguination due to a large incision made in her abdomen," the young Agent explained. "The cut was precise, likely made with a surgical instrument. Whoever killed her knew exactly what they were doing."

Laurel grimaced but nodded for Samira to continue.

"We collected various pieces of evidence from the scene. There was minimal blood at the location, which supports the theory that she was killed elsewhere. We did find tire tracks leading into the woods, and based on the impressions, we believe the vehicle was a large van or SUV."

Malik added, "We also found trace amounts of a specific type of soil on her shoes and clothes, which we've matched to a construction site on the outskirts of town. It's a potential secondary location where she might have been held before being moved to the forest."

Laurel leaned forward, her attention fully focused. "I saw that in the file, and I'm intrigued. Tell me more about the soil and the construction site. What kind of construction is happening there?"

Samira tapped her tablet, bringing up a detailed map and images of the construction site. "The soil we found on Tiana's shoes and clothes matches a specific type found at a large construction project on the outskirts of Appleman's Gap. It's a mixed-use development called Riverview that's been in progress for about six months now. They're building a combination of residential homes, retail spaces, and office buildings."

Laurel studied the images. "I've heard of it. What phase is the construction in right now?"

"They're in the early stages of the residential area," Samira replied. "Foundations are being laid, and some of the initial framing has started. There's a lot of heavy machinery on site, including excavators and concrete mixers. The soil we found is a distinct blend of clay and gravel, which is used for stabilizing foundations. It's not something you'd find just anywhere."

Malik added, "We've also noted that the site is relatively unsecured. Given its size and the amount of equipment, there are plenty of places someone could hide out or use as a temporary holding location. Security is minimal, mostly just perimeter fencing and occasional patrols."

Laurel nodded, processing the information. "Have we checked the site for any signs of recent activity that might be related to our case?"

"We did a preliminary sweep," Samira said. "We found some tire tracks that match the ones we discovered near where Tiana's body was found. There were also a few footprints that don't seem to belong to the construction workers.

We're analyzing those prints now to see if we can get a match."

Laurel's eyes narrowed as she considered the possibilities. "It sounds like this site could have been used as a staging area. If The Dark Hand was holding Tiana there before moving her to the forest, we might find more clues if we do a thorough search."

Malik nodded in agreement. "I think it's worth a deeper investigation. Detective Nolan already has a call in to the construction company to get access to all areas, including any temporary structures or trailers they have on site."

"Good," Laurel said. "I want a full team on this. We need to search every inch of the Riverview site and collect any evidence that could lead us to the baby. And let's not forget to review any surveillance footage they might have, even if it's just from the entrances and exits."

Samira made a note on her tablet. "I'll coordinate with Detective Nolan and the construction foreman. I'll get our team set up for a detailed search. We'll start immediately."

Laurel's mind was already working through the implications. "Did we get any DNA or fingerprints?"

Samira sighed. "Unfortunately, the perpetrator was meticulous. We found no usable fingerprints, and the only DNA present belonged to Tiana and her baby. However, we did find a few strands of hair that don't match Tiana's, and they're currently being analyzed."

"Alexia," Laurel said.

Samira looked at her quizzically for a moment, then her expression changed when she realized. "That's right. Baby Alexia. My apologies. I'll be sure to use the child's name."

Laurel smiled with closed lips. "Thank you. I think she deserves that much."

Malik leaned forward, his expression intense. "You're assuming our perp is male, correct?"

"Most violent offenders are."

"Eighty percent, right?" he asked.

Laurel nodded. "Around that. Why?"

"What if we're off base in our thinking? What if the person who killed Tiana and took her baby is female?" Malik asked, his tone serious.

"Go on."

Laurel was willing to listen, but Samira shook her head, seeming to dismiss her colleague's assertion.

"Think about the motive here. Why does The Cradler kidnap babies in the first place? For ransom, sure, but no ransom demand has been received in this case. Something else is going on," he said.

"Malik," Samira began, "I don't think Agent Dane—"

Laurel held up a hand to stop her. "Let him talk. No idea is a bad one right now."

"I don't know," Malik said. "Call it a hunch. Maybe I'm too young to have those."

"Nonsense," Laurel said. "A good Agent trusts their gut."

"Well, my gut tells me that we might be missing the forest for the trees, so to speak," Malik explained. "Think about Tiana—visiting a town she's unfamiliar with, while pregnant. It strikes me that a female might have had better luck in luring her to somewhere dangerous. Wouldn't Tiana have been more wary of a strange man?"

Laurel thought back to her own attack in Mount Pleasant, when the woman had seemed to be scouting for the man. Malik was onto something.

"Yes, Agent Washington, I think you're right," Laurel said. "We need to consider the possibility of a female accomplice. Let's dig into any female suspects who might have a connection to The Cradler's operation. We also need to re-interview any witnesses or construction workers who might have seen something suspicious."

Samira nodded, reluctantly agreeing with the direction. "I'll start compiling a list of potential female suspects. We'll cross-reference it with known associates of The Cradler and see if we get any hits."

"Good. Let's get to work."

Twenty

"I'VE GOT to get out of here," Cornelius mused.

He stood tensely in his safe house in Watkins Glen, New York, the blanket of snow outside providing a stark contrast to the warm fire crackling in the hearth. Someone had knocked on the door earlier, but when he answered, no one was there.

The realization that he was being watched settled heavily on him. After what had happened in South Carolina, he couldn't be too careful. The man who had attacked him at the fish fry could have ended his life. Cornelius was now on defense. There was little time to play offense when you were being chased. He needed to find a way to flip the script. Otherwise, his efforts in faking his own death would have been for nothing. Not to mention, his family was in danger.

He moved away from the door, his eyes scanning the room for any signs of surveillance equipment. His hand instinctively reached for the gun he had stashed in his waistband. He'd been pacing around the house for at least fifteen minutes—to the office, then back to the front door, mostly.

The house was eerily quiet, the only sound the occasional creak of the wooden floorboards. Cornelius checked the camera feed in the office once more. It was still disabled, confirming that whoever was watching him knew what they were doing. This wasn't just a random passerby. It was someone with a plan.

"All right, Sully," he muttered to his imaginary companion, "we need to figure out our next move."

He sat back down at the desk, his mind racing through the possibilities. Could it be The Dark Hand? He'd been informed about the suspected criminal's involvement in the murder and kidnapping case back home in Appleman's Gap. Or perhaps someone else from The Cradler's network? He couldn't afford to wait and find out.

It was time to take action.

Cornelius nodded to himself. He couldn't just sit around waiting. He needed to be proactive. He went over to the window and peeked outside. Snow had begun to fall steadily, covering any tracks that might have been left by the intruder.

His thoughts turned to his home in Appleman's Gap. He wished he could be there to help, but he knew his presence would only put his family in more danger. It was nowhere near time to reveal the fact that he was still alive. The handful of people who knew were enough, for now.

Cornelius decided it was time to move. Staying in Jimmy's safe houses was no longer an option. Someone was being tipped off to his locations. He needed a change of scenery, and he needed it fast. This time, he had to go completely off grid.

Buffalo wasn't too far, and he knew someone there who might be able to help. He quickly packed a small bag, ensuring he had essentials like the gun, extra ammunition, and cash. At some point, he'd pick up a new burner phone. Not yet.

He thought about his old college crush, Ruth Patterson, who had moved to Buffalo years ago. They'd kept in touch sporadically, and he knew she would take him in without asking too many questions. Ruth was resourceful and trustworthy, traits Cornelius valued now more than ever.

He scribbled a quick note for Jimmy and left it in the safe house, hidden in a drawer, just in case someone friendly found their way there after he'd gone. It read:

Jimmy, Had to move. Will be in touch. —C

Cornelius made sure the door was locked behind him and then headed to the garage where a blue Subaru Outback sat waiting. He'd have to be careful driving in the snow because he wasn't used to it, but he had no choice. As he backed out, he kept an eye on his surroundings, alert for any signs of the people who had been watching him.

The drive to Buffalo was tense. Every car that passed him or followed too closely set him on edge. He couldn't shake the feeling that he was being followed, but he pressed on, determined to reach Ruth's house. He and Maureen had sent her a Christmas card the year prior. He didn't remember her exact address, but he recalled that she was on North Range Road, up near Getzville. That would have to do. He'd figure it out from there.

After what felt like an eternity, including a stop at an internet cafe outside of Rochester to find the house number, he pulled up to Ruth's modest home on a quiet parcel of land. He parked around back behind the barn, just to be safe. He knocked on her door, and after a few moments, she answered, her eyes widening in surprise.

In truth, she looked like she'd seen a ghost. Because she had.

"Cornelius! What are you doing here?" she asked, stepping aside to let him in. "You're the last person I expected to see. You're ... well, you're supposed to be dead, aren't you? I sent Maureen a fruit basket after your funeral."

"I need your help, Ruth. I'm in trouble," he said, his voice low and urgent.

She nodded, closing the door behind him. "Come in, sit down. Tell me what's going on."

As they settled in the living room, Cornelius quickly filled Ruth in on the basics—leaving out the most dangerous details but giving her enough to understand the gravity of the situation.

"You always did get yourself into the craziest situations," Ruth said with a mix of concern and amusement. "But I'll help you, of course. You can stay here as long as you need."

As far as Cornelius knew, Ruth was single. She'd been married a long time ago, but after her husband passed away in a tragic boating accident, she'd sworn off men.

She was a feisty one, still fit and strong after all these years. Still pretty, too. Her straight blonde hair was cut in an angled line that grazed her shoulders while still allowing a view of her delicate collarbones and peeks of her elegant neck. Cornelius couldn't help but notice the rise of her jeans either, and the way they hung on her hips. It was a shame that the two of them had never gotten together.

"Thanks, Ruth. I don't know what I'd do without you."

Ruth smiled, her eyes twinkling with a hint of mischief. Her gaze seemed to linger on him, which piqued his interest. "Well, you always did have a way of finding trouble, Cornelius. I'm not surprised you ended up on my doorstep. I might even go as far as to say that a part of me imagined it would happen someday."

"Seriously?"

"Oh, yeah."

Cornelius chuckled, feeling a bit more relaxed in her presence. "Yeah, I guess you're right. I've always been a magnet for chaos."

They sat in comfortable silence for a moment, the crackling of the fire in the hearth the only sound in the room. Cornelius couldn't help but let his eyes wander over Ruth, remembering the times they'd shared back in college. Even though they'd never dated, he'd wished for their friendship to turn into something more. He and Maureen had been together, though, and they had been in the process of deciding how serious their relationship was going to be.

"You know, Ruth," he began, his tone playful, "I always had a crush on you back in the day. I just never had the guts to tell you."

Ruth raised an eyebrow, clearly amused. "Is that so? Well, I suppose now is as good a time as any to tell you that the feeling was mutual. I always thought you were too focused on your studies and your future to notice me."

Cornelius was genuinely surprised. "Really? I thought it was one-sided. I guess we were both a little too shy for our own good. Such a shame."

Ruth laughed, a soft, melodic sound that filled the room.

"Seems like it. If only we'd known, we might have had a little more fun back then."

Cornelius felt a warmth spread through him, a mix of nostalgia and something more. Maybe he didn't need to meet new women like Tricia and Carmen to be appreciated. Perhaps the answer to a satisfying relationship could be found in his past. That is, if he couldn't get back into Maureen's good graces.

"Better late than never, I suppose," he said. "You look amazing, by the way. Time has been very kind to you."

Ruth blushed slightly, a hint of color rising in her cheeks. "You're not so bad yourself, Cornelius. Although, I have to admit, I didn't actually expect to see you again, let alone under these circumstances. Can I get you a glass of wine?"

Cornelius wanted the wine, or a beer, but he'd learned that lesson at the fish fry. He needed to remain sober to keep his wits about him. "Life has a funny way of throwing curve-balls," Cornelius replied, leaning back in his chair. "No wine for now, thanks. But I'm glad I ended up here. It's good to see you."

Ruth's smile softened, and she reached out to place a hand on his. "It's good to see you too, Cornelius. And don't worry, you're safe here. How about some food? Have you eaten? I can cook you something."

Cornelius' eyes lit up. "I'm starving, but I must insist that you let me cook for you. It's one of my hobbies that I've recently brought back out to play. I'd like nothing more than to see a satisfied smile on your face when you taste what I make for you."

They spent the next hour in Ruth's kitchen reminiscing about their college days, sharing stories and laughter that eased the tension Cornelius had been carrying. It was a welcome respite from the constant fear and danger he'd been living with. Ruth had made a comment about how she had no quality ingredients to work with, but as it turned out, she had everything needed to make a savory beef bourguignon, a zesty arugula salad, and homemade bread. The meal was delicious.

As they moved around the kitchen, they found reasons to touch each other. The salt shaker was held between them a few seconds longer than necessary, folding the napkins was an excuse to fold their hands together, and the cramped quarters between the stove and the island gave them a reason to lean against each other for a moment.

Ruth seemed receptive to Cornelius' advances. He was certain that if he took things a step further, she would reciprocate.

"Does Maureen know?" Ruth asked, her voice slurring slightly from the wine. Just because Cornelius wasn't drinking didn't mean she had to abstain. She'd filled her glass full of a hearty red and was nearly finished.

"Know what?" he asked, his voice slow and smooth. "That I had a huge crush on you?"

Ruth laughed. "That you're alive."

He sighed. It was a touchy subject. "She does now. She's shacked up with a guy we went to high school with. Mack Roberts. She's good and mad at me."

"I'm sorry to hear that. You were always a lovely couple."

"Looks can be deceiving," he said. "We were, but we also had our fair share of struggles and disagreements. You don't always know what's happening behind closed doors. I'll admit, I wasn't the best husband."

Ruth shook her head. "Don't say that. None of us are perfect. You're a good man, Cornelius Dane. I know that much, for sure."

He shrugged. "It's true. I've had a wandering eye."

"Maybe you weren't with the right person," she replied. "Did that ever cross your mind?"

He looked deeply into her eyes, taken aback by her honesty. What if she was right? They'd known each other for so long. Back when they'd spent so much time together, he had been a young man with his whole life ahead of him. Maybe Ruth knew a better version of him. One that he'd nearly forgotten himself.

As he looked at her, he noticed her gaze fall to his lips. Women only looked at a man's mouth like that when they were thinking about what it would feel like. What it would taste like. In that moment, he knew that he could kiss her, if he wanted to. Did he?

He hesitated.

"What are you thinking about?" she asked.

"Nothing," he replied. "The last few days have been a whirlwind. That's all. Now here I am with you, eating delicious food ... admiring your beauty."

Before Cornelius could make the decision, Ruth did it for him. She leaned in, pressing her soft lips against his. A charge went through his body, as if he'd been plugged into an electric socket. This woman was remarkable. The fact that they'd known each other so well, so long ago made it all feel right.

What could go wrong?

Twenty-One

"WE'RE ON IT," Malik assured Laurel as they wrapped up their meeting and he and Samira left the conference room. "We've got agents ready to move in on a moment's notice if we get any solid leads."

"Good," Laurel said, her resolve hardening. "We need to find Baby Alexia and bring her home. And we need to make sure The Cradler and his associates pay for what they've done."

She'd barely had time to sit back down at her desk when the door to the conference room opened, and Detective Nolan walked in. His expression was as unfriendly as ever.

"Agent Dane," he said curtly.

Josh's slicked-back hair was beginning to soften as the day wore on and the products he'd used lost their oomph. It didn't look quite as much like a hair helmet anymore.

"Detective Nolan," she replied, trying to keep her tone neutral.

What she really wanted to do was get to the bathroom for a potty break. She thought about Lilly at home, hoping the pup would have a chance to relieve herself. Although they hadn't discussed it, Laurel assumed that Brad would stop by to let her out for a few minutes.

Nolan crossed his arms, looking around the room. "I hear you're planning a raid. I hope you're not planning to go in guns blazing and mess things up."

Laurel stood, facing him squarely. "We're coordinating with your team, Detective. This is a delicate operation, and we're treating it as such. We all want the same thing here: to bring Tiana's baby home safely. But all that said, no raid has been planned just yet. Where are you getting your information?"

Nolan sneered, but he didn't answer the question. "Just remember, this is my town. I don't want any more chaos because of you or your father's legacy."

Laurel's jaw tightened, but she kept her voice calm. "What are you even talking about? We're all professionals here. Let's focus on the task at hand."

Nolan stared at her for a moment, then nodded grudgingly. "Fine. Just don't screw this up."

He turned and left, leaving Laurel feeling a mixture of frustration and determination. She had no time for personal vendettas. The mission was all that mattered. Although she did wonder what had made Josh so hostile toward her. Was it something Cornelius had done?

She took a deep breath and got back to work, knowing that every second counted. The Cradler's reign of terror had to end, and they were the ones to make it happen. She had an appointment that afternoon with an OB in town, Dr. Elsa Stewart. She would already be missing work time to dip out and go, so she didn't want to waste any more.

Laurel ate lunch at her desk—a peanut butter and banana sandwich on whole wheat bread with a side of air-popped popcorn and a single hard boiled egg—then she wrapped things up and headed to Dr. Stewart's office. Luckily, no one but Matt saw her leave. He was as friendly as ever, bidding her goodbye as she walked out the front door.

"I'll be back within the hour," she said as she waved to him. "Take messages, okay?"

He nodded, happy to help.

Laurel's drive to Dr. Stewart's office was filled with a flurry of thoughts. She couldn't shake the confrontation with Detective Nolan—if that's how it should be described. Was she becoming too sensitive? His animosity felt personal, but she didn't have time to delve into his motivations. For the next hour, her priority was her baby.

The OB's office was located in a quaint, old, two-story house near the heart of Appleman's Gap. The waiting room had a soothing ambiance, with soft music playing and comfortable chairs arranged in small clusters. Laurel checked in at the front desk and took a seat, glancing around at the other expectant mothers.

Brad had offered to come with her, but she'd insisted that he stay at the police station and do what he could on Tiana's case. She assured him there would be plenty more prenatal appointments for him to attend. Besides, she was simply here to meet the doctor and find out if she'd be a good fit.

Laurel noticed a woman flipping through a parenting magazine nearby and decided to strike up a conversation to pass the time. She appeared to be here alone, too.

"Hi, I'm Laurel," she said with a friendly smile.

The woman looked up and smiled back. "Hi, I'm Simone. How far along are you?"

"About eighteen weeks. Maybe twenty. This is my first visit, so I'm not completely sure," Laurel replied. "You?"

"Twenty-two weeks," Simone said, placing a hand on her rounded belly. "Do you know what you're having yet?"

"I don't, but I have a feeling it's a girl," Laurel said, feeling a surge of happiness at the thought. "I'm planning to move back here from Washington, D.C., so I figured I should get established with a doctor in town. Appleman's Gap will be home for us."

It was the first time she'd said it out loud. That made it feel official. There was a lot to be done to move everything home from D.C., but she could hire people to help with that. More importantly, this was a huge step forward for her and Brad. If she could just get rid of Jamie somehow, things in their relationship would be good. Laurel still hated the fact that the men in her life were hiding something from her.

So, Jamie was pregnant, but who was the father? They insisted it wasn't Brad. But who? Laurel would feel so much better if she knew. Laurel wasn't the type to scheme about how to manipulate other people. Not at all. Although, maybe it was time to do just that.

"How wonderful," Simone said. "Doctor Stewart is amazing. You'll like her. And Appleman's Gap is a great place to raise a family. My husband and I moved here a few years ago, and we love it. The community is so supportive."

"I grew up here," Laurel said, "so I know exactly what you mean. My family owns Dane Family Orchards. The city has changed a lot with all the new people moving in, but I like to believe we haven't lost our friendliness or Southern charm."

"Not a bit," Simone said. "Although traffic is crazy. I'm waiting for them to widen the road out on Main Street."

Laurel nodded, thinking about her dad. As Chief of Police, he had dealt with many changes to their little hometown, ushering in a new era of growth and prosperity. Not everyone agreed with the decisions that city officials had made, but she thought they'd done a good job. She wondered how Brad would handle the changes that would inevitably come in the future. So far, it seemed like he was filling her dad's shoes and would do just as good a job.

"My fiancé is Chief of Police," Laurel said, liking the way the word fiancé sounded coming out of her mouth.

"Oh, that handsome big guy with the dark hair?" Simone asked. "He's a hottie."

Laurel blushed. She was used to women finding Brad attractive, but something about it seemed different now that he was the father of her baby.

"Thanks," she said simply, not sure what else to say.

It was nice to spend a few minutes being a regular woman at a doctor's office instead of Agent Dane. Simone had no idea that Laurel was an F.B.I. agent. It made Laurel think that maybe, if she took the leap and became a private investigator, she could live a fairly normal life. She had to admit, that sounded appealing.

As they continued to chat, Laurel felt a sense of calm settle over her. It was fun to think about the future and to hear positive things about the town she would soon call home again. Just as Simone was describing the local parks, a nurse called out, "Dane?"

Laurel stood up, ready to follow the nurse, when she noticed a young blonde woman standing up from a hidden spot behind a column. The woman's eyes widened in surprise, and Laurel felt a jolt of recognition.

"Jamie?" Laurel asked, puzzled. "What the hell are you doing here?"

Laurel had known Jamie was pregnant, too, but she was none too pleased to see her at the same OB's office. Were there others in town?

Jamie looked equally startled. "Laurel? I, um ... I'm here for my appointment."

Laurel's brow furrowed. "They called my name."

Jamie practically danced in front of her chair, she seemed so nervous. "Yeah."

"Why did you stand up when they called the name Dane?"

Jamie's face turned pale, and she glanced around nervously. "I ... I'm using the name for the baby. It's complicated."

Before Laurel could press further, the nurse intervened. "Jamie Dane, we're ready for you."

Jamie quickly walked toward the nurse, leaving Laurel standing there, bewildered. She watched Jamie disappear down the hallway, a multitude of questions swirling in her mind. Why was Jamie using her last name? And what was she hiding?

Trying to push her curiosity aside, Laurel followed another nurse who had appeared to escort her to an exam room. As she walked down the hallway, she couldn't help but feel that something significant was being hidden from her. It was incredibly obvious that something big was happening. What?

The nurse led her into a cozy exam room and handed her

a gown. "Dr. Stewart will be with you shortly. Please change into this."

Laurel nodded and changed into the gown, her mind still racing with thoughts of Jamie. As she sat on the exam table, she tried to focus on the appointment ahead. She needed to ensure that everything was progressing well with her pregnancy.

A few minutes later, Dr. Stewart, a kind-looking woman with long, dark hair and a warm smile entered the room. "Hello, Laurel. I'm Dr. Stewart. It's nice to meet you."

"Nice to meet you, too, Dr. Stewart," Laurel replied, trying to put Jamie out of her mind for now. It wasn't working.

Dr. Stewart went over Laurel's medical history and current health, then performed the necessary checks. "Everything looks great so far," she said reassuringly. "Your baby is healthy, and your vitals are good. Do you have any concerns or questions? Do you want to know the baby's sex? I'd like to do an ultrasound, anyway."

Laurel shook her head. "No, everything seems fine. No concerns. I don't think we want to know the sex ahead of time. I just want to make sure I'm prepared for the move back to Appleman's Gap and that I have the right care."

"You're in good hands here," Dr. Stewart said. "We'll make sure you and your baby have everything you need. I'd love to care for the both of you."

I have everything I need except peace and harmony with this baby's father, Laurel thought. *I swear, if he doesn't tell me the whole truth about what's going on with Jamie, I might have to kill him.*

Twenty-Two

CORNELIUS PULLED AWAY from Ruth's kiss, then quickly stood.

The last time he had kissed a woman other than his wife, it was Jamie, and she had ended up pregnant. He'd made a royal mess out of things, and the fallout hadn't even happened yet. Maureen didn't know he had a baby on the way.

He'd kissed Tricia on the side of the mouth and had been fully prepared to kiss her more deeply, but then the gunman had shown up and interrupted.

"I'm sorry," Ruth said. "That was presumptuous of me."

Cornelius put a hand over his mouth. "It isn't your fault. It's mine. I need a minute to think."

"Take your time," Ruth said, then she stood to clear their plates.

Dishes and silverware clinked softly in her kitchen sink as Cornelius began to pace back and forth in the living room. He ruminated on his situation. Could he trust himself to make good decisions when it came to beautiful women? So far, his track record on that was spotty, at best.

His eyes darted around the room, not really focusing on anything in particular, until they landed on a framed, cross-stitched piece that struck him as odd. It had two red hearts on either side of the words "The Midwife." As far as Cornelius knew, Ruth had been a middle school science teacher before she'd retired a couple of years ago.

"What's this about?" he asked. "The Midwife? Did you go into a new profession without telling me? Here, I thought I had kept up with you pretty well over the years."

Ruth stiffened, then seemed to force herself to relax again."It's nothing," she said.

Cornelius lowered his brow. "It's hanging on your wall. It must be something. Come on, you can tell me. It's just *me*."

She turned and resumed her work on the dishes. "Just a nickname," she said over one shoulder.

He thought about asking more questions, but decided to drop it. What did it really matter, anyway? He had more pressing issues to deal with.

"You're tense," Ruth said, drying her hands on a dishtowel, then walking over and placing them on Cornelius' shoulders. "Sit down. Let me give you a shoulder massage."

He opened his mouth to protest, but her soft hands felt so good on his body.

"Okay."

"Are you sure I can't get you a glass of wine? I hate drinking alone," she said.

He sighed heavily, considering it. He really wanted some wine. To relax and unwind. He'd been so stressed on the drive west. He considered the status of things.

His car was parked behind Ruth's barn, out of sight. He'd left all electronic devices at the safe house. He'd even checked the car for trackers before leaving Watkins Glen. It was clean. He didn't think he'd been followed. How would anyone find him? He was here with an old friend. A beautiful, trustworthy, old friend. Surely, he was safe enough to enjoy a glass of wine and a shoulder rub.

"You talked me into it," he said.

Ruth practically chirped with delight. "Yay!" she said. "Now we're getting somewhere."

She smiled as she padded back to the kitchen, her steps light and graceful. Cornelius watched her move, feeling a mix of unease and attraction. He tried to push away his doubts, convincing himself that he deserved a moment of peace.

Ruth returned with two glasses of red wine, handing one to Cornelius before settling next to him on the couch. She raised her glass, and they clinked together in a quiet toast.

"To old friends," she said, her eyes sparkling.

"To old friends," Cornelius echoed, taking a sip.

The wine was rich and velvety, and he felt a warmth spreading through his body, easing some of the tension in his muscles. He told himself this was different from the night of the fish fry. That event had taken place out in the open, where anyone could approach and cause havoc. Tonight, he was hidden and protected by Ruth's house. Not to mention, snow had begun to fall again. It was unlikely that anyone could see through the heavy precipitation, let alone stage an attack. The Buffalo area was known to get even more snow than Watkins Glen, thanks to the lake effect. Cornelius glanced out the front windows. It was really coming down out there.

Ruth set her glass on the coffee table and resumed massaging Cornelius' shoulders. Her touch was firm yet soothing, and he closed his eyes, allowing himself to relax for the first time in days.

"You always were so tense," Ruth murmured, her fingers kneading the knots in his shoulders. "Even back in college. I remember watching you study for hours on end, barely taking a break. You were so driven."

Cornelius chuckled softly. "I guess some things never change. I've always been driven, but sometimes I wonder if it's worth it."

Ruth's hands moved lower, massaging his upper back. "It's worth it. You've accomplished so much, Cornelius. You're a good man, despite everything."

He opened his eyes and turned to look at her, surprised by the sincerity in her voice. "You really think so?"

"I know so," she said, her voice soft and reassuring. "I always admired you, you know. Back in college, I had the biggest crush on you. I thought you were the most amazing guy. That was before I moved north and became a Damn Yankee."

Cornelius smiled, feeling a pang of regret. "I had no idea. I kid you not, I always thought my crush on you was one-sided."

Ruth smiled, her hands still working on his back. "It wasn't. I liked you a lot. But life had other plans for both of us, I guess."

"I guess."

He looked into her eyes, feeling a connection that he hadn't felt in a long time. The warmth of the wine and her touch made him forget, just for a moment, the danger that surrounded him. He leaned in closer, their faces just inches apart.

Ruth's breath hitched, and she tilted her head slightly, inviting him to close the distance. Cornelius hesitated, his mind full with more thoughts of Maureen and the mess he'd made of his life. But Ruth's presence was comforting, and he found himself drawn to her.

As their lips met again, the kiss deepened, fueled by years of unspoken longing. Ruth's hands moved to his chest, slowly unbuttoning his shirt. Cornelius felt a rush of desire and a sense of escape from his troubles. They reclined on the couch, their bodies entwined, the intensity of their kiss growing.

Ruth's hands roamed over his body, and Cornelius responded in kind, feeling the heat between them. He forgot about his worries, about the danger he was in, about everything except for the woman in his arms. He laid her all the way down on the couch, their breaths coming in short, urgent gasps.

Ruth pulled back slightly, her eyes searching his. "You seem distracted, Cornelius. You need to relax. Tell me, what have you been dreaming about lately? What would make you happy?"

Cornelius hesitated, then sighed. "I'm more relaxed than I was a little while ago, I promise you that."

"And what would make you happy?"

He traced a circle on one of Ruth's forearms with his finger. "I've been thinking about getting a black lab puppy. I know it sounds silly, but I've been talking to an imaginary dog named Sully."

Ruth smiled softly, running her fingers through his hair.

"That's not silly at all. It sounds like you need a loyal companion, someone to share your life with."

He chuckled, a hint of sadness in his eyes. "Yeah, I guess I do. I've made such a mess of things. My family, my career ... everything."

Ruth's touch became more tender, more intimate. "You've always been too hard on yourself. You deserve happiness, too. You deserve to have someone who cares about you."

He looked at her, vulnerability etched across his features. "Do you really think so? After everything I've done?"

"Absolutely," Ruth whispered, her lips brushing against his ear. "You've always been a good man. You just need to forgive yourself and move forward. You can trust me."

Cornelius felt more warmth spread through him, as if he was falling under Ruth's spell.

"I do trust you. I wish it were that easy," he said softly.

Ruth kissed his neck, her hands exploring his body. "It can be. You just have to let go of the past and embrace the present. And maybe ... embrace me."

He felt a surge of emotion, both desire and fear. He hated being so unsure of himself. What would Laurel say if she saw him in this compromising position? It had only been a few days since his daughter had lectured him about how his actions affected other people.

"Ruth, I don't want to hurt you. My life is so complicated right now."

She looked into his eyes, her gaze steady and reassuring.

"I can handle complicated," she said. "I want to be here for you. Let me in, please."

Their lips met again, the kiss growing more passionate, more urgent. Cornelius felt a deep connection, a need to lose himself in her embrace. He allowed himself to forget the weight of his responsibilities and the danger that lurked.

He made the decision. He would make love to Ruth, right there and then. Consequences be damned. He was only human, after all.

As they moved closer to the edge of giving in to their desires, a loud noise from outside shattered the moment. Cornelius sprang to his feet, his hand instinctively reaching for the gun at his waistband.

"What was that?" Ruth asked, her eyes wide with fear.

Cornelius moved to the window, peeking through the curtain. The snow-covered landscape was still and silent, but his gut told him something was wrong. He turned to Ruth, his expression serious.

"Stay here," he said. "I'm going to check it out."

She nodded, her face pale.

Cornelius moved cautiously to the front door, gun in hand. He opened the door slowly, stepping outside into the cold. The snow crunched under his boots as he scanned the area, looking for any signs of movement. Luckily, Jimmy's team had left him proper clothing for the cold weather, but he'd hurried out Ruth's door too fast to grab his coat. The icy precipitation stung his skin.

His eyes darted to the spot where his car was hidden behind the barn. It was untouched, as far as he could tell. But something felt off. He had learned to trust his instincts over the years, and they were screaming at him now.

Cornelius moved around the side of the house, checking the perimeter. As he approached the back, he saw something that made his blood run cold. The security cameras he had noticed earlier were gone. Someone had been here, and they knew what they were doing.

He hurried back inside, locking the door behind him. Ruth was waiting in the living room.

"What's going on?" she asked.

"Someone was here," he said, his voice tight. "They removed the cameras. We need to be on high alert."

"What are we going to do?"

Cornelius took a deep breath, trying to formulate a plan. "We need to stay hidden and stay quiet. Whoever is out there, they're dangerous. We can't take any chances."

Twenty-Three

LAUREL FUMED as she got into Brad's truck and drove the short distance from Dr. Stewart's office to the police station. At least, she'd avoided seeing Jamie on the way out. What a day, and it wasn't over yet.

Realizing that she should talk to someone to let off steam before she put Brad on blast, Laurel dialed Mikey's number. He picked up on the second ring.

"Hey, Sis, what's up?"

"I'm going to kill him, Mikey, I swear to God," she said.

She balled her hands into fists, then punched the steering wheel. The force caused the horn to honk loudly. An elderly gentleman sitting on a porch swing waved in response as she drove by. She waved back, unsure whether to laugh or cry.

"Whoa, slow down, killer," Mikey said. "Who are you after?"

"Brad Tate."

"Oh," Mikey said, retreating.

"Do you know what just happened to me?" Laurel asked. "You'll never believe it in a million years. Unless, of course, you're in on this charade, too. In that case, I'll add you to my hit list.

"Charade? What charade are you talking about?" Mikey sounded genuinely confused, but Laurel wasn't convinced.

"I went to my OB appointment and ran into Jamie Beck. She's pregnant, Mikey, as you know, and she was using the name 'Dane' at the office. Care to explain?"

Mikey was silent for a moment before he spoke. "I ... I didn't know she was using our last name."

"Well, she is. And I need to know why," Laurel demanded, her voice rising with each word. "What's going on? I'm so mad at Brad for not telling me the truth, I could choke him. I know he knows. I think you know, too."

Mikey sighed. "Look, I don't know everything, but I do know that Jamie's baby is going to be a Dane."

Laurel's mind raced. Her anger and confusion were mounting. "Are you saying that Ryan got her pregnant? Our little Ryan?"

Mikey hesitated. "I didn't say that, but ..."

"Oh my God," Laurel interrupted. "This is unbelievable. I guess they are close to the same age. I just never thought ... I mean ... He'll be throwing his life away, getting tangled up with the likes of her. I have to talk to Mom about this."

"Sis, wait. Maybe you should talk to Jamie directly. Get the full story before jumping to conclusions."

But Laurel was already too worked up. She was determined to put an end to the secrecy, once and for all. She hated it.

"I'll talk to Jamie eventually. I don't owe her anything. Right now, I need to get to the bottom of this with Mom. Do you think she knows?"

Mikey didn't want Laurel to call their mom. In fact, Maureen was the last person he wanted to find out about Jamie's pregnancy. He wasn't sure how to stop his sister, though. She was fit to be tied, as Maureen would say.

Laurel didn't give her brother a chance to intervene. She ended the call and quickly dialed her mother's number. Maureen picked up after a few rings, her voice cheerful, as always.

"Hi, sweetheart! How are you? Are you feeling good for your first day back to work? I'll bet you're happy as a pig eatin' slop."

Laurel had missed her mom while away in the Carolinas. She was eager to pay her a visit, once she had a little more breathing room in Tiana and Alexia's case. It was remarkable, really, how Laurel had lived in D.C. for years, yet now felt out of sorts when being away from Appleman's Gap for a few days.

As a kid, Laurel had been a daddy's girl, but that didn't mean there was any lack of love for her mother. Maureen had been there for her kids through thick and thin—all five of them. That's why Laurel knew she had to tell her mom what was going on with Ryan right away.

"Mom, you won't believe what I just found out," Laurel blurted, her frustration bubbling over. "I don't know a delicate way to say this, so I'll come right out and do it. Ryan got a girl pregnant. She's using our last name at the OB's office!"

There was a moment of stunned silence on the other end before Maureen spoke, her tone shocked and confused. "What? Our Ryan? Are you sure?"

Laurel sighed. "Well, not a hundred percent sure, but

Mikey all but confirmed it. He said Jamie Beck's baby will be a Dane. I was surprised, too, when I heard."

Maureen paused again, and Laurel could imagine the look on her mom's face. "Should I recognize that name? Jamie Beck? Sounds familiar, but I can't place it."

"She's new in town. From Alabama, I think. Or she has an aunt who lives there, anyway," Laurel explained. "She's living in Brad's carriage house."

"Ah," Maureen said. "That's it. I've heard mention of a little hussie out there causing problems for you. Want me to talk to her?"

Laurel couldn't help but chuckle. "That's sweet, Mom," she said, "but it's Ryan I'm concerned about. Stay focused, here. I think he's the father. If he is the father, his life is going to change for the worse. He'll probably have to quit school and move home, which would be a shame since he's so close to graduating with his bachelor's degree. But someone will have to support the baby. He should do the right thing, shouldn't he?"

Maureen's voice was firm as she replied, "Look, I'm sure there's more to the story. I'll talk to Ryan and figure out what's going on. Just ... take a breath, okay?"

Laurel took a deep breath, trying to steady her racing thoughts. "Yeah, okay. But this is just ... it's a lot, Mom. Jamie irks me. And I'm mad at Brad for hiding things. Again. I guess he's trying to protect Ryan. I don't know."

"I know, sweetheart. We'll get through this. Let me handle Ryan. You focus on taking care of yourself and that baby of yours."

"Okay. Call me back when you know more."

Laurel ended the call, her emotions still swirling. She had

a lot to process and even more to prepare for. Talking to her mom for a few minutes had helped, though. If Ryan had fathered Jamie's baby, Maureen would set him straight. She'd see to it that he man up and take responsibility.

Collecting her thoughts as she parked in the station lot, Laurel steeled herself for Samira's gruesome investigation images and Josh Nolan's hostile attitude. Personal issues would have to wait.

When Laurel stepped into the station, she was still distracted with everything she had learned and the conversation she had just had with her mom. She needed to focus on the case at hand, but the revelation about Jamie and the possibility that her brother might be involved was hard to shake off. Luckily, her colleagues stood ready to help.

As she walked into the conference room, she saw Malik and Samira huddled over a laptop. They looked up as she entered, their expressions a mix of concern and determination.

"Agent Dane, we've got something," Malik said, standing up and gesturing for her to join them at the table.

Laurel took a seat, ready to dive into the details. "What did you find?"

Malik exchanged a glance with Samira before speaking. "Kanesha Sneed stopped by the station again while you were out. She and Paul found something at her apartment that might be a lead."

Laurel's interest was piqued. "What did they find?"

Samira turned the laptop screen toward Laurel, showing her an image of a business card.

"They found this business card wedged in the crack of the

sofa," she explained. "It's from a real estate firm, but here's the thing—it doesn't exist."

Laurel frowned, studying the card. "What do you mean, it doesn't exist?"

Malik pointed to the screen. "We ran a search on the name and address of the firm, but there's no record of it anywhere. It's like it was made up. The woman in the picture doesn't show up in any preliminary searches either. We have someone at Headquarters digging deeper."

Laurel immediately thought of her friend Della and how she'd offered to assist in any way she could. "I have a friend who could help us, too," she said. "Special Agent in Charge Della Brady."

"That's her!" Samira said, getting excited.

Her enthusiasm was contagious. It made Laurel remember the thrill of solving cases when she was younger and less experienced. Although the work was still a rush, those early cases in a young Agent's career are something very special.

Laurel's brows raised. "Agent Brady is the person at Headquarters digging deeper?"

Samira and Malik both nodded.

"She's filling in for Agent Paulson this week," Malik said.

"Good," Laurel replied with a nod. "We're in capable hands."

"Seems that way," Samira agreed, practically grinning.

Laurel's heart skipped a beat as she leaned in and looked closer at the photo. "This woman ... she looks familiar. Do we have any idea who she might be?"

Samira shook her head. "No, but the card was found at Kanesha's apartment, and it's possible she could be connected to the case. The fact that there's no record of the firm is suspicious."

Laurel leaned back in her chair, her mind working through the possibilities. "Did Kanesha or Paul recognize her?"

"They didn't," Malik said. "But Kanesha mentioned that the card wasn't there before the incident with Tiana. It's possible it was planted."

"Kanesha also said that she'd been trying to convince Tiana and Paul to move to Appleman's Gap. It's possible that Tiana was interviewing realtors in preparation," Samira added.

Laurel nodded slowly. "And that so-called realtor could have been showing Tiana a homesite in Riverview, where the construction dust was present."

"Exactly."

"We need to find out who this woman is and why her card ended up at Kanesha's apartment. It could be a clue to where Baby Alexa is," Laurel said.

Samira clicked through a few more images on the laptop. "We're running facial recognition to see if we can get a match, but it might take some time. In the meantime, we should follow up on any leads we can find about this fake real estate firm. At minimum, someone printed the business card. It looks like it was done by a professional press."

"Okay, let's split up the tasks. Malik, you keep working on the facial recognition and see if you can dig up anything about the real estate firm. Samira, you and I will go through the rest of the evidence from the crime scene. Maybe there's something we missed."

Just as they were about to get started, Malik's phone

buzzed. He glanced at the screen and then looked up, his expression serious. "Agent Dane, you're going to want to see this."

He handed her the phone, and she read the message. It was from one of their tech analysts, confirming that the woman in the photo had been flagged in a database. She had multiple aliases and was linked to several suspicious activities across different states.

Laurel's eyes widened as she read the name believed to be the woman's real identity: Ruth Patterson.

"That's her," she said, her voice barely above a whisper. "She's an old friend of my dad's from college. Could she be connected to The Cradler's syndicate?"

Malik and Samira looked at her, shocked. "Are you sure your dad knew her?" Samira asked.

Laurel nodded. "Positive. We need to move fast. She could be the key to finding Tiana's baby."

Twenty-Four

RUTH MOVED CLOSER, her eyes wide with fear but her touch still lingering on his arm. "What if they come inside? We're not safe here, are we?"

Cornelius felt a surge of protectiveness for Ruth, but also a growing unease.

"We'll be fine. Just stay calm and stick with me."

He didn't know if that was actually true, but it would do no good to alarm the woman.

Ruth nodded, but her eyes held a glint of something he couldn't quite place. He led her to the living room and handed her a blanket that was draped over the back of a nearby easy chair.

"Wrap up and stay warm," he said. "I'll check the other exits and make sure everything is secure. Can you think of any reason for someone to remove your security cameras? No technician installing new service or anything?"

"No."

Ruth took the blanket and wrapped it around herself, sitting on the couch. Cornelius moved through the house, checking doors and windows, ensuring everything was locked. He kept glancing back at Ruth, his mind full of conflicting thoughts. Something didn't add up. He reminded himself that she was an old, dear friend. He believed he could trust her.

As he returned to the living room, Ruth offered him a reassuring smile.

"Thank you for looking out for me. I feel safer with you here," she said.

Cornelius sat down beside her, still on edge. Ruth reached out and touched his hand.

"We'll be all right," he assured. "I just need to stay vigilant. If anything happens, we need to be ready to move quickly."

"You've been through so much. You deserve some peace. Maybe we should try to relax for a moment, just to clear our heads."

He looked at her, seeing the sincerity in her eyes. She seemed to genuinely care for him, just like she had back in college. He was beginning to feel groggy.

"I wish it were that simple, Ruth. There's so much at stake," he said sadly.

Ruth leaned in closer, her voice soft and soothing. She seemed to want him, and she didn't seem concerned that someone might be lurking outside.

"You've always been a protector," she said. "But even protectors need rest. Let me help you find some peace, even if it's just for a moment."

Cornelius felt a strange mix of comfort and suspicion. Was she really trying to seduce him? Was she simply lonely up here in the cold, living alone without a man to keep her warm at night? Or did she have an agenda?

If he were being honest with himself, he had wondered about Tricia Bowers, too. She'd seemed a little too eager to fill him with beer that night at the fish fry. Or maybe he was being paranoid.

He wanted to trust Ruth, to believe in her intentions, but something nagged at the back of his mind. He took another sip of his wine.

"You're right, my friend. Maybe just for a moment," Cornelius said.

Ruth moved closer, her body pressing against his. Her breasts were firm for a woman of her age. She'd taken good care of herself. Cornelius was aroused.

"You know," she said seductively, "we could be more than friends. Just let go. Let go of the worries, the fears. I'm here with you."

He felt his tension ease slightly, the wine and her touch working together to further dull his senses. He was tired from the drive and the stress of having been on high alert all day. As they sat together, he tried to push away his doubts and focus on the present.

It would soon be dark outside, and it felt like time to settle down and cozy up. Cornelius had nowhere else to go for the night. Not unless he contacted whoever was filling in for Jimmy and asked to be taken to a new safe house. That didn't seem wise because someone was clearly leaking information about his whereabouts. Perhaps it had something to do with Victor Garton and the threat to expose him. Cornelius wasn't sure, and his senses weren't sharp enough to make sense of it.

Suddenly, a faint sound broke the silence—a baby's cry,

distant but unmistakable. Cornelius froze, his eyes widening in shock.

"Did you hear that?"

Ruth's expression didn't change. "Hear what?"

He stood up, his head spinning slightly. Was he imagining things? He didn't think so.

"A baby. I heard a baby crying."

Ruth shook her head, her eyes narrowing.

"Cornelius, you've been under so much stress. Maybe you're just imagining things," she said, reading his mind.

But Cornelius knew what he had heard. He moved towards the source of the sound, his heart pounding. As he reached the back of the house, the crying grew louder, more distinct.

"It sounds like it's coming from the barn," he said, his words beginning to slur.

His head felt heavy. His eyes drooped. He shook in an attempt to stay awake and alert.

Grabbing his coat this time, he exited the back door of Ruth's humble home and stepped out into the snow on the back deck. As he looked toward the barn, he saw the unmistakable glow of a warm light.

"That wasn't on before," he said to himself.

He stumbled forward, the sounds of the baby's cries growing louder. He walked as quickly as he could, making his way to the barn. He reached for his gun, but it was no longer tucked into the back of his waistband.

"Shit," he said. Then "Who's there?"

There was no answer except for the hoot of an owl. He turned to face it, remembering the heron and the cardinal. Were these birds some kind of sign?

It took a moment, but he finally spotted the snowy owl perched on a wooden fence a short distance away. Its white feathers blended in with the snow, making Cornelius wonder if it was really there or if he was hallucinating. He remembered hearing that some cultures believe an owl visits shortly before a person is to die. Was it a Native American tribe who thought so? Was it true? Or had that come from another novel he'd read?

He certainly hoped this owl wasn't a sign of impending doom. He had so much more to do in life. He looked into the animal's eyes, saying a silent prayer for protection. The owl hooted once more in response, offering a small comfort.

Cornelius steeled himself and moved on. If this was his day to die, at least, he wouldn't go down without a fight.

When he arrived at the barn, he opened a door, revealing a staircase leading down to a basement. It looked creepy, like something out of a horror movie. Was his mind playing tricks? The baby's cries continued.

Ruth's voice was suddenly behind him, cold and sharp. Gone was the warmth and friendliness of a short time prior.

"Cornelius, stop," she said.

He turned to see her standing at the top of the stairs, her face a mix of concern and something else—something darker.

"Ruth, what's going on? Why is there a baby down here?"

Ruth stepped forward, her demeanor shifting.

"You don't understand," she said. "You need to leave it alone. Trust me."

He shook his head, determined to find the truth.

"I can't do that. There's something you're not telling me."

As he descended the stairs, stumbling along the way, the

baby's cries grew louder, echoing off the walls. Cornelius' mind raced. His instincts screamed that he was walking into a trap. Ruth followed, her footsteps echoing ominously.

"Please. Just come back upstairs. We can talk about this. I wanted us to have a nice meal and … some intimate time."

"What do you mean? You didn't know I was coming until I showed up at your door. Did you?" he asked.

He reached the bottom of the stairs and saw a small, dimly lit room. In the corner, a makeshift crib held a tiny, crying baby with rich brown skin and big brown eyes. She couldn't have been more than a week old. Cornelius' heart broke at the sight.

He turned to Ruth, his voice trembling with anger and confusion. He didn't think Ruth had ever had children, which meant no grandchildren, either.

"What is this, Ruth? Whose baby is this?"

"I tried to protect you," Ruth said, her face twisting. "But you had to keep digging."

Before he could react, the effects of the drugged wine hit him full force. His vision blurred, his limbs felt heavy, and he stumbled, barely able to keep his balance. He heard the door at the top of the stairs creak open and the sound of footsteps approaching. Whoever was coming sounded big.

Cornelius tried to reach for his gun, remembering that it wasn't there. Ruth must have taken it when he was distracted. His movements were sluggish.

He turned to Ruth, betrayal etched on his face. He could no longer trust her, that much was clear.

"Why, Ruth? Why did you do this?"

Ruth's expression hardened.

"Simple. You were a loose end. The Cradler needed to tie

up loose ends. He knew if you were placed anywhere nearby, you'd come to find me. And here you are."

As he struggled to stay conscious, Cornelius heard the footsteps draw closer. The baby's cry was now a haunting backdrop to his growing dread. The last thing he saw before darkness took him was the cold, calculating look in Ruth's eyes.

THE NEXT MORNING, Laurel returned to her desk in the conference room, ready to start the day.

She'd worked late the evening before, and she hadn't mentioned anything to Brad about seeing Jamie at Dr. Stewart's office. By the time she'd fallen into bed, she'd just wanted to sleep. Baby Alexia needed her full attention.

Laurel glanced at the pile of files on her desk, feeling the weight of the investigation pressing down on her. She took a deep breath and opened the first file, diving into the details. Every clue, every piece of evidence, was crucial.

Just as she was getting into the rhythm of her work, the door opened, and Malik walked in. "Morning, Agent Dane," he said, holding a cup of coffee.

"Morning," she replied, grateful for the refreshment, but careful not to drink too much caffeine now that she was pregnant. "Decaf?"

"Just the way you like it, boss."

"Thank you, Agent Washington," she said. "Anything new?"

Malik nodded, setting the cup down on her desk. "Actually, yes. We got a hit on the facial recognition. The woman on the business card? It's definitely Ruth Patterson."

Laurel's eyes widened. Part of her didn't want it to be true. She'd learned a long time ago that being in law enforcement meant some rude awakenings when it came to people you thought you knew. It was still a jolt to the system when it turned out that someone wasn't who they seemed.

"My dad's old friend. Damn. What do we know about her?"

"Like we said yesterday, she's been linked to several suspicious activities across different states," Malik said, pulling out a file. "And she has multiple aliases. We believe she's deeply involved in The Cradler's syndicate."

"What makes you think that? Women aren't usually violent criminals, and they don't typically harm babies."

"I know, but I told you I had a hunch," Malik said proudly. "Seems like I was right. We've tracked communications that show her in contact with The Cradler's network, dating back several years. She was a science teacher who retired about that long ago. She must have needed something to fill the time."

"This is big, Malik. We need to find her and see what she knows about Baby Alexia."

Malik nodded. "I agree. We've already put out an alert and are coordinating with other agencies. Local police knocked on her door in Buffalo, New York, but no one was home. Don't worry. We'll find her."

"They'd better do more than knock," Laurel said. "Do we have enough evidence to justify a thorough search?"

Malik nodded. "Working on it."

Just then, Samira walked in, her expression serious. "Agent Dane, Agent Washington, we've got another lead. Kanesha and Paul remembered something else. They found a receipt from a hardware store in town. It's dated the day before Tiana was killed."

Laurel stood up, her pulse quickening.

"What are you thinking?" she asked.

"Let's get over there and see what we can find," Samira said. "Maybe Ruth was there, or someone who knows her."

Laurel and Malik nodded, grabbing their jackets. As they headed out, Laurel's phone buzzed. It was a text from Della.

Update on your dad. Call me ASAP.

Laurel's heart sank. She quickly dialed Della's number as they walked to the parking lot.

"Della, it's me. What's the update?"

Samira and Malik tried not to eavesdrop, but Laurel knew she needed to stay vigilant about what she said out loud. Neither of the young agents knew that her dad was alive.

Della's voice was calm but urgent on the other end of the phone. "Your dad left the safe house Jimmy placed him in."

"What? How could that be?"

"I don't know," she replied. Laurel could hear the concern in her friend's voice. "He must have thought he had no other choice. He went completely off grid, leaving no trace. I have agents on the way to do a more thorough search, but as best we can tell, all he left was a note for Jimmy saying he'd had to move and a bucket list of sorts with things he wanted to do before he died."

"Aww," Laurel said, pausing to put a hand over her heart.

She remembered what her dad had said about feeling like he would die soon, and it terrified her. She had just gotten him back after thinking he'd been dead. She didn't think she'd make it through the real thing. Especially now that she had a baby on the way. Cornelius Dane needed to meet his grandchild.

"I'm sorry to be the bearer of bad news, friend," Della said as a dark sedan pulled into the station parking lot and came to a stop.

Laurel looked up at the car. A beautiful woman with long, dark hair was driving, and she looked awfully familiar. In an instant, recognition settled over Laurel. It was Della, right here in Appleman's Gap.

Seeing that Laurel had spotted her, Della ended the call and got out of the car. She rushed forward to hug her friend.

"You devil, you," Laurel said with a smile. "I didn't ask you to come down. What are you doing here?"

Della shrugged. "I know. But sometimes friends need to do things without being asked. It seemed like you could use a hand down here."

Laurel smiled from ear to ear as she wiped a happy tear from her eye. "You're the best, Della. The very best."

"Aww, it's no big deal," Della said. "What *is* a big deal is this cute baby bump you're sporting. You look adorable."

"You think so?"

Della nodded. "Abso-freakin-lutely. You're positively glowing!"

"You can compliment me more at home tonight," Laurel said. "You're staying with Brad and me."

"Nonsense. I don't want to be a bother. I have my eye on

an Airbnb with a clawfoot tub. It's cute as a button," Della said. "Your little hometown is darling!"

Laurel started to object, but there was a lot going on. It might be better if Della stayed somewhere else. Jamie was enough of a distraction.

"Well, if nothing else, you had better come hang out in the evenings," she said. "I seem to remember being promised your homemade empanadas."

"Of course."

Samira and Malik were standing awkwardly nearby, trying not to intrude. There was a break in the conversation, so Laurel and Della finally looked their way.

"Are you going to introduce me to your Agents?" Della asked.

"Of course," Laurel said, clearing her throat and getting back to business.

"Agent Brady, meet Agent Samira Aziz and Agent Malik Washington."

They all shook hands.

"Are they good eggs?" Della asked, her long hair blowing in the breeze.

Laurel had always thought her friend looked more like a runway model than an F.B.I. agent. Except for the icy stare she could levy when needed, that is.

"They are," Laurel said. "They're green, but they're good."

Samira and Malik smiled like proud kids whose teacher had just complimented them. She had.

"Can I speak openly in front of them?" Della asked.

Laurel knew instantly that what Della had to say was

about her dad. From the sound of it, Samira and Malik would need to know that he was alive. He might need their help.

Laurel nodded.

Della turned to the young agents, looking them straight in the eye. "Let me remind you that the information you're about to hear is classified. I expect complete confidentiality. Do not breathe a word of it to anyone other than the four of us and Agent Paulson. Do you understand?"

"Yes, ma'am," Malik said.

"Yes, I understand," Samira echoed.

Della nodded, too, then dove right in.

"We've traced the car Cornelius Dane was driving to a location near Buffalo, New York. He's off the grid, but we're closing in. We believe he might be with Ruth Patterson. We've learned that there's a woman involved in The Cradler's syndicate who's known as The Midwife. We suspect Ruth might be her."

Samira's eyes went wide. "Wait. Cornelius Dane ... who died last year?"

"One and the same," Della replied. "We've been protecting him while he worked undercover to bring The Cradler's syndicate down, but he left the safe house yesterday morning without any electronic devices. We think he's in trouble."

The tone became somber as Samira and Malik came to realize the implications for Laurel.

"Agent Dane, I'm sorry," Malik said. "We'll do everything we can to find him."

"Yes," Samira added. "We will."

"A team is on the way to Ruth Patterson's New York property as we speak. If he's there, we'll find him," Della said.

Laurel felt a surge of determination. She appreciated having three of her fellow Agents working alongside her to find her dad.

"Keep me posted," she said to Della. "We need to nail Ruth Patterson, and fast. My dad's life might depend on it. We're heading to follow up on a lead now. I'll check in with you later."

Della nodded. "Go. I'll make myself comfortable in there until you get back. Anyone I should watch out for?"

Samira piped up before she thought better of it. "Detective Josh Nolan seems to have it out for Agent Dane."

Della smiled approvingly. "Noted. Thank you, Agent Aziz."

They said quick goodbyes, their resolve strengthening. The short drive was tense, each of them lost in their thoughts, but united in their mission. They had to find Ruth, find Cornelius, find Baby Alexia, and bring everyone home safely.

As they pulled into the parking lot of the hardware store, Laurel's phone buzzed again. It was a message from Brad.

> Call me when you get a chance. We need
> to talk.

Laurel sighed, knowing she couldn't avoid the uncomfortable conversation forever. But for now, she had to focus on the task at hand.

She silenced her phone and stepped out of the car, ready to uncover the truth.

Twenty-Six

CORNELIUS WOKE to the sound of the baby crying. His head throbbed, and his vision was still blurry, but he could make out the dimly lit room around him. The basement was cold and smelled of damp earth. He was lying on the floor, his hands and feet bound with thick rope.

He struggled to sit up, his body protesting with every movement. The baby's cries were louder now, more desperate. The poor child sounded hungry. It had been years since he'd had a newborn, but a parent never forgets what a hungry baby sounds like.

Cornelius forced himself to focus. He had to save that child, no matter what it took. He had a hunch she was Tiana Sneed Douglas' baby—the one Laurel had told him about. That meant that she had been brutally ripped from her mother's womb as Tiana was left for dead. It was hard to imagine a fate more cruel.

It didn't make sense how the baby had ended up here, in Buffalo. When Cornelius had rescued his grandson, Baby Jasper, a couple of months prior, the infant had been in

Middle Tennessee. All he could think was that The Cradler's reach must extend far beyond what any of them had realized.

The door at the top of the stairs opened, and two large men descended. One of them held a gun, while the other carried a duffel bag. They moved with the confidence of men who had done this many times before.

"Well, well, look who's awake," the man with the gun sneered. "Welcome back, Cornelius. We've been waiting for you."

Cornelius glared at him, his anger giving him strength. "Who are you? What do you want?"

The man laughed. "What do we want? We want you to suffer. We want you to know that you failed. That baby was supposed to be part of a much bigger plan, and now you've ruined everything. Really, though, you walked right into our trap."

Cornelius's mind raced. He had to find a way out of this. He looked over at the baby, who was still crying in the corner. "Let the baby go. She's innocent."

The man with the duffel bag opened it and pulled out a syringe. "Innocent? Maybe. But she's leverage now. And you, Cornelius, are going to watch as we use her to send a message."

Ruth appeared at the top of the stairs, her face twisted with a mix of regret and determination. "Don't make this harder than it has to be, Cornelius. Just stay down, and it will be over quickly."

Cornelius' heart pounded in his chest. He couldn't let this happen. He struggled against his bonds, feeling the ropes dig into his skin. He had to get free. He had to save that baby.

As the man with the syringe approached, Cornelius saw

his chance. With a burst of strength, he kicked out, knocking the syringe from the man's hand. The other man raised his gun, but Cornelius was already moving, using his bound feet to sweep the man's legs out from under him.

It was strenuous for a man in his seventies, but adrenaline fueled his efforts.

Ruth screamed as the man with the gun fell, his weapon clattering to the floor. Cornelius lunged for it, grabbing the gun with his bound hands. He aimed at the man with the syringe, his vision still blurry but his aim steady.

"Stay back," Cornelius growled. "Let the baby go."

The man with the syringe hesitated, then slowly raised his hands. "All right, all right. Just calm down."

Cornelius kept the gun trained on the man as he moved toward the crib. He reached in, his hands shaking, and lifted the baby into his arms. She was tiny and fragile, her cries softening as he held her close.

Ruth stepped forward, her face pale. "Cornelius, please. Just let us go. You don't understand."

Cornelius' voice was cold. "Oh, I understand perfectly. You betrayed me. You betrayed that innocent child. And now, you're going to pay. The Midwife, huh? What a name. What a sorry excuse for a life."

He moved toward the stairs, keeping the gun trained on Ruth and the two men. His head was still spinning, and he knew he wouldn't last much longer. But he had to get the baby to safety. He had to protect her.

As he reached the top of the stairs, he heard sirens in the distance. Help was on the way. He just had to hold on a little longer.

Cornelius stumbled out into the snow, the cold air biting

at his skin. His coat had been removed at some point and the sun had set. The air was bitter.

The baby was quiet now, her tiny body warm against his chest. Cornelius looked back at the barn, seeing Ruth and the men standing in the doorway, their faces twisted with rage.

"Stay back," he warned. "The police are coming. It's over."

Ruth's face crumpled, and she fell to her knees. "Cornelius, I'm sorry. I never wanted this."

But it was too late for apologies. Cornelius turned and began to walk away, his legs shaky but his resolve strong. He would get the baby to safety. He would make sure she was protected.

As the sirens grew louder, Cornelius felt his strength waning. He stumbled, his vision going dark. But he held on, focusing on the tiny life in his arms. He had to keep going. He had to save her.

Just as he was about to collapse, he saw flashing lights approaching. The police were here. He had made it. Cornelius fell to his knees, cradling the baby in his arms as he lost consciousness.

The last thing he heard was the sound of footsteps running toward him, and then, once again, everything went black.

Cornelius drifted into unconsciousness, the cold snow pressing against his skin. His mind faded in and out of a dreamlike state, filled with memories from his past. He saw himself and Maureen in the early days of their marriage, laughing and dancing at their wedding. Relatives—including his dear parents—who were long gone flashed vivid in his mind's eye. The sight of them, along with the sound of

Maureen's laughter, was like a soothing balm, comforting and familiar.

"Hi, Mom and Dad," he said, maybe out loud. He couldn't be sure.

He reached for his mother's cheek, her soft skin crinkled yet full of life. She smiled sweetly as she looked at her son with pride. She had always doted on her boy. In fact, it was because of her that Cornelius had become such a good father himself. It was also because of her that Cornelius felt so protective of children, in general. His mother was patient and kind, and she made her kids feel completely loved.

He turned to his father, who rushed forward and enveloped him in a tight hug. The old man's eyes shone brightly with admiration for the son he'd often said he'd wished for. In his dad's embrace, Cornelius felt understood, his transgressions forgiven. His dad was a good man, and he was proud of his boy. It felt good for Cornelius to belong in such a fundamental way. It felt good to be accepted.

As Cornelius scanned the crowd, he saw his grandparents, several of his aunts and uncles, and a few friends who had passed on to the other side. Even Raven, his beloved black lab from years before, was there, wagging her tail madly. He bent down and scratched her on the head, praising the pup for being such a good girl.

It was like a welcome home party. A reunion of the best kind. And Cornelius was the guest of honor.

He felt content in this place, like he could stay. The scene in front of him was much like ones he'd enjoyed as a child. The people there to welcome him had been the very same folks around to welcome him to this Earth as a baby, too.

He floated in a state of bliss without a care in the world.

The scene shifted and he dreamt of when his children were young, playing in the backyard of their home in Appleman's Gap. Laurel was just a little girl, running around with Mikey, Maggie, Hazel, and Ryan. Sarah was there, too, playing with Laurel and enjoying herself. The sun was shining, and Maureen was sitting on the porch, watching them with a smile on her face. Cornelius felt a warmth in his heart, a stark contrast to the cold reality he was currently enduring.

In his dream, he picked up a young Laurel, twirling her around as she giggled. He could see Maureen's loving gaze, and he felt a profound sense of happiness. These were the moments he cherished the most, the moments that made all the hardships worthwhile.

Suddenly, an awareness broke through to him, and he felt an overwhelming longing for his life. He wasn't ready to leave it just yet. Although, he wasn't sure the choice would be his to make. He was on some strange cosmic roller coaster, and it didn't seem like he was the one turning the dials.

His awareness shifted. He found himself back in the present, the reality of his situation seeping into his consciousness. He heard the distant wail of sirens, growing louder with each passing second. He felt the cold bite of the snow, the weight of the baby in his arms, and the pain from his injuries.

He could hear voices now, muffled but urgent. Strong hands lifted him, and he felt the baby being gently taken from his grasp. He tried to speak, to tell them to be careful with her, but his voice wouldn't come. He wanted to see the baby safe, to know she would be all right, but his vision was darkening once more.

Cornelius slipped back into unconsciousness, his mind returning to the dream. He saw Maureen again, this time holding a newborn baby, Laurel. The love and joy on her face were indescribable. He wanted to stay in this dream forever, where everything was perfect and safe.

In and out of consciousness. In and out. It was becoming hard for Cornelius to tell what was happening.

The real world began to intrude again as he felt himself being placed on a stretcher. The sounds of the police and paramedics surrounded him, their voices urgent and professional. He felt the warmth of a blanket being wrapped around him, the secure feeling of being lifted and moved to an ambulance.

In his dream, Cornelius saw his family gathered around a Christmas tree, the kids opening presents with wide-eyed excitement. Maureen was there, looking as beautiful as ever, her eyes full of love and pride. It was a scene of pure happiness, unmarred by the darkness and danger that had plagued his recent years.

As the ambulance doors closed and the sirens began to wail again, Cornelius felt a deep sense of peace. He knew he had done everything he could to protect that baby, just as he had always tried to protect his own family. The faces of his children and Maureen filled his mind, giving him strength and comfort.

He drifted into a deeper unconsciousness, the pain and cold fading away. His last thought was of Maureen, hoping she would forgive him for everything, for all the mistakes and the secrets. He hoped she knew how much he loved her and their children. They were his everything.

The ambulance raced through the night, the paramedics working diligently to stabilize Cornelius. As they approached Buffalo General Medical Center, they communicated his condition to the waiting medical team, preparing them for his arrival. Cornelius remained unconscious.

His body and mind needed rest.

In his dreams, he stayed with his family, the love and warmth of their presence a sanctuary from his harsh reality. Cornelius held onto the memories, finding solace in the moments that had defined his life and given it meaning.

Twenty-Seven

HOURS LATER, as the team's investigation wrapped up for the day in Appleman's Gap, Laurel found herself back at the station. The evidence they had gathered at the hardware store was promising. She felt a surge of pride. They were making real progress.

Laurel, Malik, and Samira gathered in the conference room. The atmosphere was charged with anticipation as they prepared to review the findings. Laurel spread the evidence out on the table, carefully examining each piece.

"All right," she began, looking at her team. "Here's what we have so far. The receipt from the hardware store was key. It's dated the day before Tiana was killed and shows a purchase of several items including a heavy-duty tarp, duct tape, and a specific brand of concrete mix."

Malik leaned in, nodding. "The concrete mix is a match to the dust we found on Tiana's shoes and clothes. It's used at the Riverview construction site. This ties our suspect to both locations."

Samira held up a small plastic bag containing a broken piece of a trowel. "We found this in the store's parking lot, near where the surveillance footage shows a woman matching Ruth Patterson's description loading the items into her car."

Laurel took a deep breath, feeling the pieces of the puzzle click into place. "The trowel piece matches the type used with that brand of concrete mix. It's circumstantial but adds weight to our theory."

Malik added, "We also found partial fingerprints on the tarp packaging that match Ruth's. She's been careful, but not careful enough. Our team couldn't ID the partial prints at first, but once they knew to compare them to Ruth's, we got a hit."

Laurel nodded, her mind racing. "Okay, so we have her at the hardware store, buying items that were likely used in the crime. But what about the motive? Why would Ruth, a retired teacher, get involved in something so heinous?"

Samira pulled out a folder and handed it to Laurel. "We did some digging into Ruth's background. She had a significant amount of debt after her husband's death. It looks like she might have been desperate for money. We also found communication between her and The Cradler, suggesting she was being paid to perform certain 'services' for the syndicate."

Laurel's eyes narrowed as she flipped through the documents. She still had a hard time wrapping her mind around the fact that this woman was an old friend of her dad's, but it was all becoming crystal clear.

"So she was part of The Cradler's network, but acting independently," Laurel said. "This wasn't a random act of violence. It was a calculated move to gain favor and money. Who would imagine that dissecting frogs and fetal pigs in a middle school science lab would evolve into cutting unborn babies from their mothers' wombs?"

Malik continued, "Yes, and it gets worse. We found emails where Ruth, under the alias 'The Midwife,' discussed acquiring babies for The Cradler. Tiana and Baby Alexia were her targets."

Laurel felt a chill run down her spine. "That explains why Tiana was murdered and the baby kidnapped. Ruth was delivering on her promise to The Cradler. But why bring the baby to Buffalo?"

Samira answered, "We think she was planning to sell the baby to someone connected to The Cradler's syndicate. The email chain indicates a transaction was being arranged. Buffalo was a convenient location for the exchange, especially since that's where Ruth lived. I suppose she thought Appleman's Gap was far enough away from Buffalo that she wouldn't be caught."

Laurel clenched her fists, anger boiling within her. "We need to bring her in. This woman can't get away with what she's done."

Malik nodded. "We've already issued a warrant for her arrest. Local authorities should have already reached her home. Hopefully, Agent Brady has an update."

Laurel took a deep breath, feeling a sense of grim satisfaction. "We have her. The evidence is solid. Ruth Patterson, The Midwife, is responsible for Tiana's murder and the kidnapping of Baby Alexia. We're going to take her down. Good work, Agents. I'd say we make an excellent team."

The door to the conference room opened, and Della stepped inside, her face grim but determined.

"Agent Dane, we need to talk," she said, closing the door behind her.

Laurel nodded, sensing the urgency. "What's up?"

Della took a deep breath. "We've located your dad. He's in bad shape, but he's alive ... for now. F.B.I. and local police raided Ruth Patterson's property in Buffalo. They took her and two men into custody. They found your dad and Baby Alexia. The baby had, apparently, been kept in the basement under Ruth's barn."

Laurel's heart skipped a beat. "Is my dad okay?"

"He's in critical condition, but he's stable. They've got him in the ICU at Buffalo General Hospital. It was touch and go for a while, but he's expected to pull through."

Laurel felt a wave of relief and worry wash over her. She couldn't lose her dad now, not when they were so close to bringing The Cradler's syndicate down. Not to mention, she wanted many more years with him in her life. The feelings of anger she'd held about him and his weakness for women melted away as she considered what it would be like to lose him, for real this time.

"Thank you," she said, her voice choked with emotion.

Della nodded. "I've arranged for a private jet to take you, Brad, Mikey, and Maureen to Buffalo. We need to move quickly."

Laurel wasted no time. She gathered her things and called her family. Within the hour, they were on the plane, racing toward Buffalo. They'd thrown some clothes into bags and left Lilly with Mack Roberts. Thankfully, he had been gracious enough to offer to care for the pup and wish Maureen well on the journey, saying he understood why she needed to go and be by her husband's side. Maybe he wasn't such a bad guy, after all.

As they arrived at the hospital, the gravity of the situation hit Laurel. Della stayed in the waiting room. The rest of them were ushered into Cornelius' room, where he lay unconscious, hooked up to various machines. The steady beep of the heart monitor was a constant reminder of his fragile state.

Maureen gasped when she saw him, tears streaming down her face. "Oh, Cornelius," she whispered, taking his hand. "You're too weak to whip a gnat."

Mikey stood beside his mother, his jaw clenched, trying to hold back his emotions. Brad put a comforting arm around Laurel, his presence a source of strength.

Laurel stepped forward, her eyes brimming with tears. "Dad, we're here," she said softly. "You're going to be okay."

Cornelius stirred slightly, his eyes fluttering open for a brief moment. "Laurel?" he croaked, his voice weak.

"I'm here, Dad," she said, squeezing his hand. "Mom, Mikey, and Brad are, too. You saved that baby. She's okay."

"Top notch work, Chief," Brad said to his soon-to-be father-in-law. "Your undercover days are done. This is all over the national news. You're a bonafide hero."

"Maureen isn't mad?" Cornelius asked.

"Mad about what, you old coot?" Maureen asked.

"About me having my own baby on the way?"

He managed a small smile before drifting back into unconsciousness. Laurel looked at the doctor, her expression questioning.

"He's stable for now," the doctor said. "But it's going to be a long road to recovery."

Laurel nodded. "Is he loopy from the medicine?"

Brad and Mikey glanced at each other, finally tired of keeping Cornelius' secrets.

Mikey was the one to say it out loud. "It's not the medicine talking. Dad is the father of Jamie's baby. Not Ryan. That's why Jamie used our last name at the OB's office. That's why Brad is letting her stay in the carriage house—as a favor to Dad."

"Oh, my stars," Maureen said, covering her eyes.

To her credit, she took a deep breath and collected herself, her resolve strengthening.

Laurel did the same.

No one had the heart to be angry at Cornelius, given the state he was in. They'd almost lost him. They would find a way to get through this, together.

As they sat by Cornelius' bedside, the conversation turned to lighter topics, trying to keep the mood positive. They talked about Baby Alexia, about the case, and about the future.

Kanesha called at one point, thanking Laurel and her team profusely for solving her sister's murder and bringing her baby niece home safely. Laurel was delighted to have been able to do that for Kanesha, who was becoming a true friend. She knew that once Jimmy got the news, he'd feel the same way. Solving crimes was satisfying work.

When Cornelius began to stir again, Mikey brought up the bucket list they had found.

"Dad, they found your bucket list," he said, his voice thick with emotion. "We read it, and we're going to help you complete it."

Cornelius didn't respond, but the steady beeping of the heart monitor was becoming a comfort. He was still with them.

A nurse who had been checking Cornelius' vitals looked up, her eyes twinkling. "Did I hear you mention a bucket list?" she asked as she made a note on his chart. Snow fell softly outside the window.

Laurel nodded, smiling. "Yes. The number one item on it is getting a black lab puppy."

The nurse's smile widened. "Well, isn't that something? My sister breeds black labs, and she recently had a litter that's ready to go to their new homes. They're just an hour or so away. I could arrange for one to be brought here."

Laurel's heart lifted. "Really? That would be amazing."

"A boy. His name is Sully," Cornelius managed, a tear in his tired eyes.

The nurse nodded. "Chief Dane, consider it done."

TO BE CONTINUED.

Get Book 3 in the series, *Fate That Twists Her.*

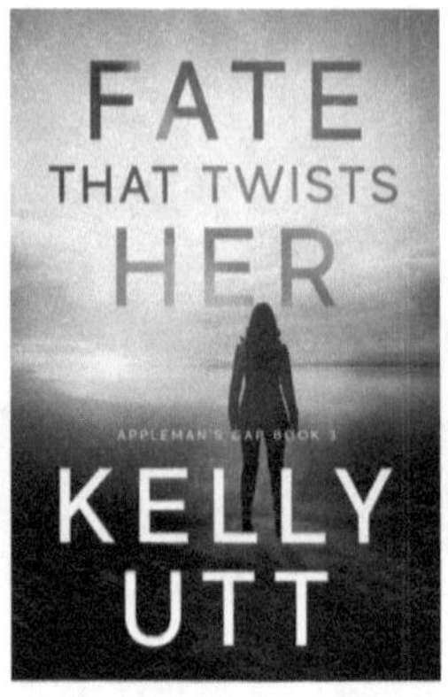

* * *

Join Kelly's mailing list for updates and bonus content, including your free Kelly Utt short story!

Enjoy this book?

A NOTE FROM AUTHOR KELLY UTT

Did you enjoy this book? You can make a big difference.

Honest reviews of my books help bring them to the attention of other readers.

If you've enjoyed this book, I would be very grateful if you could spend just five minutes leaving a review (it can be as short as you like) on the book's retail page where you purchased and on Goodreads or BookBub.

Thank you very much.

STANDARDS OF STARLIGHT BOOKS
KELLY UTT

Kelly Utt writes emotional, pulse-pounding suspense, family saga, and women's fiction novels. The stakes are high. The twists and turns will keep you on the edge of your seat.

Kelly was raised by a dad who would read a book, ask her to read it, too, and then insist they discuss it together, igniting her passion for life's big questions. That passion is often reflected in her novels, giving them a depth which leaves readers wanting more and thinking about her stories long after the last lines are read.

Kelly holds a Bachelor's degree in psychology from the University of Tennessee, Knoxville and a master's degree in interactive media and communications from Quinnipiac University.

She lives in Nashville, Tennessee with her husband and sons. She also writes novels with one of her sons as the combined pen name Christopher Kelly.

www.kellyutt.com